INSATIABLE

A Billionaire Romance

By Lucy Lambert

About This Book

I am NOT like those other women!

When Vaughn Ward sets his sights on a woman, she always ends up in his bed - crying out his name that night and cursing it the morning after. The billionaire playboy has an unquenchable thirst for sexual conquests.

Not me, though. I am a professional. But as the youngest member of C&M Advertising firm, it's my job to get to know our most important client. To get to know exactly what he wants from us... and how I can provide it.

I can resist his charms, his stares, and his flirts. I know his reputation. I won't be another notch on his bedpost.

But the longer I spend around him, the more he seems determined to take me. Use me. Consume me.

And the more I find out about him, the more I want him too...

***

"Don't be. I'd like to ask you a question," I said.

"You're asking permission?" she asked, eyes flicking back at me for a moment.

"That surprises you?" I replied.

"It does. As near as I can tell, you say whatever is on your mind regardless of the content."

"Sometimes," I agreed. There was a firecracker under

the surface of this one, I could tell. She needed someone to light her fire.

"So what is it?" she said, her curiosity overcoming her reservations.

I tugged her closer, our bodies almost touching. This close, I could see the hint of freckles on her cheeks. I bet they came out so nicely in the summer sun. I bet she hated them so much, hated how girlish they made her look. I wanted to kiss them.

She smelled nice, too. Nothing fancy. Maybe just the barest hint of perfume. It begged me to lean in closer, to graze her skin with my lips while I breathed deeply of her.

I could also feel her begin trembling. But what sort of tremble was it? Barely-suppressed attraction? Annoyance? Both? I still couldn't tell.

"What would you do if I kissed you right now, junior executive Quinn Windsor from Callaghan & Montblanc?"

Her breath caught in her throat, and her eyes widened so that I could see the whites. Her mouth opened and closed a couple times. I considered leaning in and trying my luck then and there. I couldn't get my mind off those freckles.

Her palm became hotter against mine. But she still didn't make a move to pull it away.

Her face flushed again, bringing out those freckles even more. My heart palpitated. I knew I had her. I knew I had to have her...

***

Don't forget to sign up for my mailing list to get access to all my new books and sales! :)

Chapter 1

VAUGHN

"Vaughn!" Stacey cried out, her bare, glistening breasts heaving.

I ran my lips down the soft skin of her throat, moving my mouth between those breasts. I watched her nipples crinkle and stiffen in delight, and I smiled against her skin.

I didn't think there was anything sexier or more arousing than a beautiful woman crying out your name in the middle of passion.

Her naked body writhed beneath me on the big, king-sized hotel bed, her hands grabbing at the sheet, pulling it into her fist and tugging the corner out from under the mattress.

And I kept going lower. I couldn't believe the heat coming off her.

In between groans, Stacey managed to say, "But... what... about... your meeting?"

I kissed the inside of her left thigh, then let my lips trail closer to their ultimate destination. She started trembling. I loved how she always started trembling right before. I stopped short.

"I don't care about the meeting. The only thing I care about right now is you. And how loudly you're going to scream my name…"

I let my hot breath run out over her quivering flesh.

"Vaughn!" she screamed again, her back arching up off the mattress again. I smiled.

I was an artist and Stacey's perfect body was my canvass. My masterpiece. A slanted bar of light came in through the heavy curtains, leaving a slash of brightness across her stomach.

You couldn't, and shouldn't, interrupt an artist in the middle of his work. Especially not for some meeting.

It's an important meeting, the thought buzzed at the back of my head, lighting in my thoughts like an annoying fly that I could shoo away momentarily but would come back to distract me soon thereafter.

So I concentrated all the harder on my current task. On the warm, smooth feeling of Stacey's skin. On the sharp intake of her breath through clenched teeth when I touched her with my lips or my tongue *just so*.

It helped. Soon, I didn't think of the meeting anymore. Only of the beautiful woman who shared the bed with me, begging me not to stop, pleading with me to take her over the edge.

I slid my hands up over her thighs and she grabbed them both, squeezing even while she screamed.

The more she enjoyed it, the more I wanted her, the hungrier I became. Soon, I couldn't resist sliding my body up along hers. I paused only long enough to grab the foil wrapper off the nightstand.

She kissed me as I entered her. Soon, our bodies moved as one. Stacey kept looking into my eyes, switching from one to the other, searching, questing.

"Vaughn…" she groaned, and I knew that she was close. I moved faster, harder, my heartbeat picking up.

She tried speaking again, but I didn't let her. And soon she couldn't say anything at all, the pleasure overrode all conscious thought so that all she could do was go rigid beneath me, her snug grip on me tightening so much that I couldn't help gasping.

She arched up again, exposing her long, slender neck. I kissed it, setting my teeth against her sensitive flesh. I was the predator and she my prey.

And then an incredible shock moved through my body, too.

"Stacey…" I groaned, the pleasure almost too much to bear, verging on pain. Then it ended, all too soon.

I rolled off her, lying on my back beside her, staring up at the tiles in the ceiling. That slant of light coming in through the window was a diagonal bar running across my chest and then down across her hips.

I loved the sweet smell of her sweat, and the sound of her deep, gulping breaths as she tried to recover some of herself.

No, not love, I thought. I hated that I'd used that word in relation to Stacey. It gave me a tight, unpleasant feeling across the front of my stomach that soured the pleasant post-sex afterglow.

It was just a slip, I told myself. A slip using that word in relation to Stacey: *love*. But it was also too late, and I knew it. Already, I just wanted to get out of there. My suit, a dignified Armani lying in a not-so-dignified heap beside the bed, called to me, urged me to pull it on and run out the door.

Her hand quested across the mattress, seeking and finding mine. She squeezed my fingers, and I didn't return the gesture.

"Hey," Stacey said, rolling onto her side so that I could see the provocative swell of her hip and the hourglass shape of her toned body.

"Hi," I said, ignoring those pleasant sights. I could hear the huskiness in her voice, and part of me knew what was coming. We'd been seeing each other for half a year now, and it had come up several times, but I'd always managed to avoid it.

Not now though, I knew.

"That was fun," I said. I hoped to divert her.

"It was better than fun, Vaughn," Stacey said, kissing my bare shoulder. Her lips were hot against my skin. She took her hand from mine and put it on my chest, then slid her fingers down, tracing them through the small dips between my abdominals.

It was nice. I wanted her to stop.

"Good. Nothing like a workout to work up an appetite. Room service?" I suggested. I threw my legs over the side of the bed and stood up, facing away from her.

3

"I love you, Vaughn," Stacey said.

In the darkness, I hoped she didn't see the way her words made my go rigid, made my shoulder hunch. My heart did a terrible dance in my chest. *No, no, no,* I kept thinking.

I liked Stacey so much. Why did she have to go and do that? Why did she have to say that?

"Vaughn?" she said. I still didn't turn to face her. I heard her sit up, heard her begin gathering the large sheet around her body. I was going to miss that body. "Did you hear me? I love you."

I felt her come up behind me. She put her hand on my shoulder and I knew she could feel the tension inside of me. "Don't you have something to say?" she asked.

"Yeah," I said, "That's... nice."

Her fingernails dug into the meat of my shoulder and I winced. "*That's nice?*" she said, spitting the words back at me. I didn't have to see her to know that anger and hurt contorted her beautiful face.

And here it comes, I thought. I knew this was going to happen. It always did. I had just been hoping that maybe things would last a little longer between Stacey and me before the inevitable happened.

But if there was one lesson I learned after becoming wealthy, it was that no amount of money could buy you additional time.

Chapter 2

QUINN

I kept crossing and uncrossing my legs beneath the table. I'd grown bored of the view of historic downtown Boston offered by the large bay window on the other side of the conference room.

And the air conditioning was too cold. For the fifth time in as many minutes, I checked my watch. I tried doing it with some tact, holding my wrist down below the level of the table and pulling the cuff of my jacket back to steal a glance.

Apparently, it wasn't hidden enough.

"The client is never late, Miss Windsor."

My eyes immediately went to the speaker, who sat beside the head of the table. "Of course not, Mr. Callaghan," I replied, my cheeks heating up.

Mr. Callaghan was a senior partner at the firm. He had a strong nose, black hair only now graying at the temples, and a suit that cost more than I made in half a year at Callaghan & Montblanc.

I'd only ever spoken to him once before, and that was at my promotion ceremony. I felt nervous around him. I hated feeling nervous. Nerves resulted in mistakes, and I couldn't afford making any.

Aside from Mr. Callaghan and myself, three other people sat around the long, rectangular table. I didn't know any of them; they were all Mr. Callaghan's assistants.

Normally, he didn't take on business personally anymore. He tended to leave that to people like me, junior executives. Except this wasn't just any client or company. This was Vaughn Ward.

I glanced over at the projection screen. There were a bunch of mock-ups and concept art for our proposed ad campaign displaying the logo for Ward's company, Phoenix Software.

Slides that we should have been through half an hour ago, when this meeting was supposed to start.

Mr. Callaghan stood up and started pacing up and down the room, walking past the decorative mantle and the antique clock that sat on it. It caught his eye on one pass.

"Miss Windsor, please go and see if perhaps Mr. Ward requires some assistance. You know the room number?"

"Yes, sir," I said, standing up a little too quickly so that I almost lost my balance, catching myself on the table.

I hate being nervous! I could feel Mr. Callaghan's eyes on me. I wonder if they disapproved of my suit. It was a skirt suit, the only one I owned. I knew Mr. Callaghan liked the old ways best. Old ways like women in skirts instead of pants. "I'll go check right away."

I hurried from the room, both eager to get out from under his eyes and annoyed at having to go check on Ward.

I went down the lavish hallway leading from the conference room of the Langham Hotel, making my way to the elevators.

I knew which room Ward was in because I'd made the arrangements for his stay here. I made it to the elevators and hit the button to call one, taking a moment to brush a few stray strands of hair off my forehead.

C&M had comped Ward this stay. The man was a billionaire. *Couldn't he afford his own hotel room?* That was a thought I needed to keep to myself if I wanted to keep my job.

The elevator was just as opulent as the hall, and it was fast.

I started down another hall. This one lined with doors. Though not so many as I was used to finding in hotel halls. *They're suites,* I remembered. Nothing but the

6

best for Vaughn Ward. I didn't even have to look at the numbers to find his room.

I didn't have to look because of the yelling. Something inside told me that it was Ward's room.

My pace slowed. *How am I supposed to handle this now?* I wondered. I'd originally intended on knocking on the door, hoping that Ward might answer and then come down with me. Now it sounded like knocking might put me right in the middle of whatever was going on in there.

There were two voices doing the yelling. A man and a woman. Though the woman's voice dominated.

I crept closer, the words becoming more distinct.

"That's nice? What the hell does that mean, Vaughn?"

"It means like it sounds. It's nice." A male voice, made deeper by its passage through the door.

I hadn't realized that he'd brought his girlfriend, too. And the thing was, I couldn't remember her name.

I do a lot of research before new assignments. Research on our clients so that I can do the best possible job. Except I always try and keep it as professional as possible. I stick to the stock reports, the business headlines. That sort of thing. And that means staying away from the supermarket checkout tabloids.

And I had to admit that in this case it was difficult to stay away from the popular pieces. Vaughn Ward was quite the character, to put it politely. The kind of guy who seemed to date a new model or actress every couple months while somehow also increasing his company's share of the market.

"I can't believe you!" the woman said. Something, probably an expensive something, crashed and shattered on the floor. I winced.

And then I crept closer to the door. Curiosity, I guess. It's not every day you get to hear a billionaire get into a domestic dispute.

I cringed, second-guessing myself. What, was I going to press my ear to the door next? Maybe try to get a peep through the keyhole?

No, I decided, *I'll go back down and tell Mr. Callaghan that Ward is... indisposed. Yeah, that's a good word for it!*

I didn't relish being the bearer of bad news. Especially not bearing it to one of the owners of the firm. But what else could I do?

Then the door to Ward's room opened. "Oh!" I said before I could stop myself.

A beautiful, if dishevelled woman stood in the darkened doorway, looking at me. Her blonde hair was in disarray. She'd pulled on her dress without bothering to zip it up, and wore only one heel. The other dangled from her hand.

For a moment there I felt the pure hatred and shock in her eyes fix on me.

"Don't go, baby," Ward said, coming around the bed, sidestepping the spray of shattered glass on the carpet. He was shirtless, I saw. In nothing but a pair of plain cotton boxers.

My first impression of Vaughn Ward was that he was handsome. Possibly the most handsome man I'd ever seen who wasn't being projected on a movie screen. Dark hair, smoky eyes, the perfect amount of stubble darkening his jaw. And tall.

Not only that, but a handsome-and-he-knows-it kind of guy. The kind of full-of-himself man who thinks he's God's gift. The kind of man I always stayed away from in high school, college, and everything after that. Tried to, anyway. They were trouble.

It wasn't a very good first impression. The beautiful blonde blocking the doorway looked at me with wet eyes, her pretty lips pulled into a grimace. I felt like I should tell her I was sorry, but for what, I had no clue.

"Good luck," the pretty blonde said.

"I... uh... pardon me?" I replied, my eyes kept trying to stray back to that semi-nude figure in the darkness behind her. *Keep it professional!*

She smiled, then. More a grimace, I guess. Full lips pulling back, nothing touching her eyes.

"Stacey, come back. We can talk about this," Ward said. I noticed then how tousled his hair looked. And the bedclothes were all kicked down and balled up. *Oh*, I thought.

Stacey squinted, keeping her eyes fixed on me. "That would be *nice*, wouldn't it, Vaughn?"

"Hey, come on, don't be that way," Ward said.

And then Stacey looked at me like she saw me for the first time, one pump still hanging from her finger. "You better watch out, girlie, or Vaughn might be *nice* to you, too." She said it low enough so that only I heard it.

Behind her, Vaughn frowned, a small wrinkle forming on his strong brow.

"I'm not sure what you mean," I said, wishing that I hadn't done so well on my last assignment to earn this big "opportunity" of working on new material for Ward.

Then Stacey pushed past me, walking lop-sided down the hall. I watched her odd gait until she disappeared into the elevator. A cold sweat had started on the small of my back while I wondered just what I'd gotten myself into.

Then I noticed that Vaughn Ward stood in the doorway in front of me, leaning out so that he could watch Stacey go.

There couldn't have been more than a few inches between us. I could smell him, then. There was something fresh in his smell, something clean about his sweat.

Heat rushed up into my cheeks and I backed up a couple steps. Ward noticed me, then. I tried not to notice that his eyes were a deep, chestnut brown full of a warmth I wouldn't have expected.

"The meeting?" he prompted. Then his eyes made a quick flick up and down my body. *Why the hell did I have to wear this stupid skirt suit today?*

Be professional, followed quickly on that thought's heels. I knew that if I played it cool with Ward, that if I toed the line, I would impress Callaghan and get on with my career.

That was it, I knew. Ward was a stepping stone, that was all. A beautiful, tall, sculpted, nice-smelling stepping stone whose eyes make me want to smile.

I think my knee-jerk physical attraction to him made me like him even less.

"Yes, the meeting. We... we have everything set up for you down in the conference rooms. Mock-ups of some TV commercials and a few banner ads placed on specific sites targeted to certain demographics that we feel will..."

He held up one hand to silence me, one corner of his mouth cocking up in a crooked smile. "Sounds good. I'm going to hop in the shower. Worked up something of a lather..." he said, clearing his throat and tossing a look over his shoulder at the dishevelled bed, "Come on in. Grab a drink out of the mini bar. I'll be out in a few minutes."

"No, thank you..." I started, intending to tell him I'd go tell Mr. Callaghan he'd be down shortly. Except Ward grabbed my wrist and pulled me inside.

The door swung shut behind me, locking me inside with Ward, locking me away from the comforting safety of the hall with its elevators and emergency exits.

"Would you like me to call someone to check on Stacey?" I said.

Just for a second, that roguish veneer of his cracked. His crooked smile faltered and he ran one hand up the back of his head, squeezing the dark hair there.

Quick as it came, it went. He smiled again, "Don't worry about her."

Normally I didn't like intruding on other people's business. However, nothing about this situation could be called normal, I thought. Besides, the nerves along the front of my stomach were practically singing.

"So you're going to let her go? Just like that?" I said.

Vaughn, who'd been turning to go take his shower,

paused. He looked at me. There was a bar of light coming in through the window and it sliced across his bare torso.

He shrugged. "Just like that. Women come and go…" he glanced over at the bed and then amended his statement with, "Pun intended. Have a drink."

I frowned at his back as he walked into the washroom. The hiss of water followed soon thereafter. *Pun intended? What an asshole!* I thought.

Still, in the back of my mind, I couldn't help wondering what he was like. I shook my head, *It doesn't matter what he's like, because he's a jerk.*

I'd been standing so stiffly I hadn't noticed until my back started complaining. Without thinking, I almost sank down onto the foot of the bed. "Yeah, let's not do that."

I almost sat down in a nice wingback beside the mantle but stopped myself. It would be just my luck for Mr. Callaghan to send someone else up here to check on *me* only to find me relaxing.

If that happened, he'd probably bump me from the job and give it to Trish. And I wasn't about to let that happen. Trish, another junior exec from the firm, would love to see me taken down a peg or two.

"You seem a little young to be at this meeting."

I jumped at the sound before realizing that Vaughn hadn't bothered closing the door to the bathroom. Steam crept out along the floor.

He was just standing in the shower stall, naked, the water sluicing down his body. I blushed, even though from here I couldn't see him.

He seemed so open, like he couldn't be embarrassed. I was used to normal people. Normal, polite people who closed their bathroom doors and who didn't make lewd puns to girls they just met.

I guess being famous and having bank accounts with sickening numbers of zeroes by the balance took away that sort of propriety, though.

"Still there?" Vaughn said again.

"Y… yes," I said. I didn't know if it was the steam from the shower or my own body temperature rising. Whichever it was, it was too hot in there.

Am I allowed to tell a client that they're wasting time? Part of me wanted to. Especially after seeing how distraught that girl Stacey had been.

Vaughn Ward needed someone to put him in his place. But that someone couldn't be me, I knew. One word of any lip to Mr. Callaghan and I'd be lucky to be working in the mail room.

Then the water stopped hissing. Ward emerged from the steam in nothing but a towel. Not wearing a towel, just holding one up to his face while he dried his cheeks and chin.

At least it fell down far enough to cover everything up.

"Oh, I'll just wait in the hall," I said.

"Stay. I insist," Ward replied. I turned away from him just as he tossed the towel to the bed. *Does he have no shame?*

"You do look young," he said. I could hear him pulling on his clothes, "You must be good at your job."

"I am," I replied. I bristled at the compliment. I didn't want any compliments from him.

"Good. Hey, you probably know who handled booking the room for me I'll bet. Do me a favor and tell them I prefer staying at the Harbor. This place is a bit… tacky for me. No accounting for taste, right?"

My eyebrows tried climbing off my forehead. Who did this guy think he was? *One of the richest, most eligible bachelors in the world. A man with so much influence he could make sure you don't work in any first world country again if he so chose,* my brain answered my rhetorical question.

Shut up, I shot back at myself. He was just another entitled, rich, handsome, womanizing jerk.

So I put on my best smile and turned around. Ward was hopping around on one foot, trying to pull his slacks up. He saw me looking and sat down heavily on the bed.

He smiled in a bashful way I was certain just about any woman with a functioning set of ovaries would find endearing and charming. I wasn't just about any woman, though.

I guess even rich jerks put their pants on one leg at a time.

"Yes, actually, I do know. I know because the person who handled your accommodations was me. And no, there isn't any accounting for taste," I said, giving him a pointed look before turning to face the corner again.

Behind me there was only silence. I could feel him looking at me. *Oh God, Quinn, what did you do? You didn't really just say that, did you?*

But I did just say it, I knew. My knees started trembling, cool anxiety flooding my stomach. I have no idea why I said that. I wasn't like that. I wasn't that sort of person. There was just something about Vaughn Ward that brought out the worst in me.

And I'd only met him a few minutes ago!

I braced myself, waiting for him to tell me that he meant to inform my boss of my attitude.

He laughed instead. It was a rich chuckle. "Now I can tell why you have this job," he said. I heard him pull his zipper up.

I bristled some more, somehow upset that he wasn't upset with me. He didn't react or behave at all like I expected. I didn't like that. I liked predictable, dependable.

"I guess you'll know better for next time, then. Let's get going. I think we're pretty late!" Ward said, chuckling again. He walked over to the door and pulled it open, light spilling in from the hall.

I hated how good he looked in that suit. I hated him holding the door open for me, waving me out with one hand.

Chapter 3

VAUGHN

Every second step I took, I thought about Stacey. I ached deep inside when I recalled the hurt look on her face, when I recalled how I reacted to her confession of her feelings.

I reacted like I always did. With humor. With pushing away. I couldn't help it. They were automatic defense mechanisms that kicked on whenever something like that happened. As inevitable as the ebb and flow of the tide over in the Boston harbor.

The too-young executive girl walked in front of me, and I couldn't help letting my eyes slide down her slate-gray skirt-suit. I admired the way it outlined her body, going in at the waist and flaring in again at the hips.

She had her sandy-blonde hair done up in a serviceable bun, and I caught myself wondering what that hair might look like waving freely around her shoulders.

I had to admit that I found her interesting. I intimidated her, I could tell that. Except she didn't clam up or just act afraid like so many others did. I mean, she actually had the nerve to talk back to me about my joke about the hotel. There weren't many people who'd do that.

I smiled at that recollection. Yes, I liked this girl. And thinking about her kept my mind off Stacey. And all the ones that came before Stacey who'd had similar experiences.

We got to the elevators and she jabbed at the button. "We have a number of proofs to show you, as well as some test footage for a new commercial," she said, keeping her eyes on her reflection in the brushed steel elevator doors. "I think you'll be pleased."

"With what I'm paying your firm, I'd expect nothing

less," I replied.

Her shoulders stiffened and I grinned. It tickled something inside me to get a rise out of her.

"Yes, well, you get what you pay for," she replied. The elevator doors opened and she went inside. I followed. She stood in the opposite corner, her eyes fixed on the dial counting down the floors.

I was still grinning from her reply. I leaned back against the wall, hooking my thumbs in the pockets of my jacket. In the normal light of the elevator I got a better look at her.

I liked the front as much as I liked the back. She wore a minimal amount of makeup. She was pretty in that normal way that made me think immediately of the phrase "*the girl next door.*"

But she tried to downplay her looks, I noticed. That lack of makeup, the serviceable hairstyle, the plain if well-fitting suit. She was a young woman determined to get by on the merits of her skills and talents rather than a pretty face and nice eyes.

"I expect nothing less than the best," I said. "Which is why I was surprised at your age."

I couldn't stop myself from looking at her lips. I wondered how soft and smooth and warm they might feel against mine. Part of me recognized this as my usual defense mechanism, my usual avoiding of the feelings for the last girl by moving onto the next as quickly as possible.

The rest of me didn't care.

"I know what I'm doing, Mr. Ward. I'm perfectly capable of taking care of your needs." She still hadn't looked away from the dial.

My grin widened, "Oh, I know you are," letting my tone convey the implication.

When she realized what I meant, her cheeks turned a rosy red that made me ache inside.

"Mr. Callaghan himself has taken the lead on handling your needs, we value your business so much. I'm sure you'll benefit from his decades of experience," I said.

I laughed again. I liked this one. Cheeky. And I could see her inner struggle playing out across her face. That desire to remain professional warring with her wit.

The flush in her cheeks deepened and I knew that she hadn't been expecting laughter as a response. That was good. I liked surprising people, liked looking at things from angles people didn't expect.

I attribute a good 80% of my success to that trait.

"You know," I said. "You haven't actually introduced yourself yet. I find that distinctly unfair, since you know who I am."

"Mr. Ward, everyone knows who you are. In fact, we're rather counting on that fact for a few of our proposals. Which Mr. Callaghan will be explaining in just a few minutes."

I sucked a breath in through my teeth. *Ouch*. I could feel the teeth in that remark going right for the jugular. I had to say, I was enjoying myself. Women always wanted to get closer to me, to learn more about me, to talk to me.

The woman standing in the corner across from me looked like she wished she could slide through the wall of the elevator and disappear. It was refreshing.

And it was the opposite of what she wanted from me, I knew. I never could resist pressing people's buttons. "Still, a real professional would introduce herself to her client."

She winced and I knew I found her soft spot. This one was all work and no play. But my God, I wanted to see her at play so bad.

She swallowed, dragging her eyes from the dial and over to my face. I fixed my most charming smile to my lips, the one I knew went straight to my eyes. Women always went crazy over my eyes.

"I'm Quinn Windsor, and I'm a junior executive with Callaghan & Montblanc Publicity and Marketing." With more than a little reluctance, she held out her hand. Her nails were plain and well-groomed, I noticed.

I reached out and engulfed her hand in mine. Her skin was warm and dry, which I found surprising. I was so used to clammy, nervous handshakes. "Quinn? That's an unusual name."

"So is Vaughn," she replied. I could tell she wanted to pull her hand back, but was too professional to try an experimental tug.

"It's good to be unusual. It gets you noticed," I said.

She breathed a little too sharply on her next breath and I knew I found myself another nerve.

This one didn't want to be noticed. At least, not for some things.

"I'll have to take your word for it, Mr. Ward," she said.

"Vaughn," I replied. Her eyes kept straying up to mine, then taking in that smile. I liked it when she looked at me. The trouble was that I couldn't tell if she reciprocated.

I thought that maybe there was some mutual attraction there, but I couldn't be certain. It was intoxicating. That flush in her cheeks was intoxicating. The way her lips parted ever so slightly as she breathed was intoxicating.

"You know," I said. "I think I'm usually pretty good at reading women. But I can't quite get a bead on you."

She looked away, fixing her gaze on the dial. We'd be out of the elevator soon, I knew. "Sorry to disappoint, Mr. Ward."

The way she turned her face showed me her profile. I let my eyes run over her face. *Girl next door, indeed.*

"Don't be. I'd like to ask you a question," I said.

"You're asking permission?" she asked, eyes flicking back at me for a moment.

"That surprises you?" I replied.

"It does. As near as I can tell, you say whatever is on your mind regardless of the content."

"Sometimes," I agreed. There was a firecracker under the surface of this one, I could tell. She needed someone to light her fire.

"So what is it?" she said, her curiosity overcoming her reservations.

I tugged her closer, our bodies almost touching. This close, I could see the hint of freckles on her cheeks. I bet they came out so nicely in the summer sun. I bet she hated them so much, hated how girlish they made her look. I wanted to kiss them.

She smelled nice, too. Nothing fancy. Maybe just the barest hint of perfume. It begged me to lean in closer, to graze her skin with my lips while I breathed deeply of her.

I could also feel her begin trembling. But what sort of tremble was it? Barely-suppressed attraction? Annoyance? Both? I still couldn't tell.

"What would you do if I kissed you right now, junior executive Quinn Windsor from Callaghan & Montblanc?"

Her breath caught in her throat, and her eyes widened so that I could see the whites. Her mouth opened and closed a couple times. I considered leaning in and trying my luck then and there. I couldn't get my mind off those freckles.

Her palm became hotter against mine. But she still didn't make a move to pull it away.

Her face flushed again, bringing out those freckles even more. My heart palpitated.

"I…" she started. Her eyes bounced around the cramped space of the elevator, unable to stay still.

Then the elevator dinged, the doors sliding open. I groaned inwardly. *Just a few more seconds,* I thought, *a few more seconds was all I needed.*

Quinn looked out the door and saw no one waiting in the lobby. Then she turned back to me, leaning in. Unable to help it, my heart rate picked up. A tingle ran down the front of my stomach.

"I'd slap you so hard you'd have to explain the hand

print on your cheek for the next week," she said. Then she tugged her hand out of mine and wiped it on her jacket. "For me and for that girl, Stacey."

Then she smiled and stepped out of the elevator, "Please follow me, Mr. Ward."

Her mention of Stacey hit me in the gut like a hard-knuckled fist. I stood there, gaping at her until the elevator doors started closing again. She had to reach in and trip the sensor so that they'd re-open.

My expression seemed to satisfy her, and I knew she thought this whole thing was over.

It wasn't.

So I smiled, tugging at my jacket to get it back in its proper place on my shoulders, and stepped out, "Lead the way."

Chapter 4

QUINN

Thank God that's over! I thought, yanking open the glass door to my condo building. I lived up in the North End on Clark Street. It was a nice building, with good views of some of the historic sections of the city.

I liked having my own place. I hated having a mortgage. But it beat renting, and besides, it made me feel more like an adult.

Although with how the day went I wasn't certain for how much longer I could afford said mortgage.

I fished my key fob out and knocked it against the sensor of the inner door. The deadbolt shot back and I walked into the mailroom. The sound of the door closing and locking behind me was the best thing I'd heard all day.

I don't know if it had been out of revenge or what, but Ward had really laid into me in the meeting. He hadn't let Mr. Callaghan get a single word in.

Every slide Ward pressed me for more details. After viewing the rough cut of the commercial he'd asked me if I'd been the one to cast it, a reference to his displeasure with my having him booked at Langham instead of the Harbor.

By the end of it, I'd been getting dirty looks from everyone else there, like I was costing C&M a huge account.

"You'll be hearing from me soon," Ward had said to Mr. Callaghan at the end. Ward hadn't smiled once throughout the whole meeting, his handsome face looking like it had been chipped from stone. It contrasted so sharply with his behavior before that.

Mr. Callaghan, normally composed, had shooed everyone from the room as soon as Ward had left. I wouldn't be surprised if I went to the office on Monday and got called in for at the very least a dressing down, if not getting handed my pink slip then and there.

I checked my mail, sorting the junk into the recycling bin without really thinking. *God damn Vaughn Ward*, I kept thinking. I hated him so much. Right from the first time I set eyes on him.

And he asked to kiss me! The nerve! Clearly being a rich and famous bachelor had gone to his head.

I slammed the little door to my mailbox shut and huffed my way down the hall. How could one man be so infuriating? So beautiful and infuriating? I didn't mean to add that second part.

But I had to admit it, grudgingly. You could hate someone and still admit they were attractive, right?

Before I could get to the elevator the doors opened and two young children, a boy and a girl, both sandy-haired and freckle-faced, popped out.

"Quinn!" they both screamed when they saw me.

"Hey, guys!" I replied, dropping down to my knees.

Alexander and Charlie were brother and sister. Alexander was nine and Charlie seven. They both rushed into my arms. They both smelled of fresh soap, and Charlie's long red head tickled at my nose.

"Watch out, or they might not let go," Mary said as she came out of the elevator. She was their mother, and she had the same red hair. She looked a little more tired than usual, the darkness below her eyes detracting from her striking features.

"Maybe I'll just hold on, then!" I said, wrapping my arms around their waists and standing up. They squealed as they left the ground. I groaned. "You guys are getting too big for this!"

I set them down, wincing and thinking I should up my workout from twice a week to three times down at the GoodLife on the corner.

"Kids, go wait by the door," Mary said. The kids

went, grinning back at us over their shoulders.

Mary came closer to me. She really did look tired. "Quinn… I hate to ask, but do you think you could watch them for me tonight? I had to take another late shift. And I just finished a double in time to go pick them up from school…"

She tried carrying on, but I held up my hand, "Not a problem. Send them over whenever you want to; I'll be home all night."

She put her hand on my shoulder. "You're a lifesaver."

"Seriously, don't worry about it. I love seeing them," I said, giving Mary's elbow a reassuring squeeze. My heart went out to that woman.

"Kids! You're going over to Quinn's tonight, ok?" Mary said.

"Woo!" Alexander and Charlie called back from the door.

"And if you're both good, I know I have some mac & cheese we can have for supper," I added.

Both their faces lit up and I couldn't help grinning. They were great kids.

I started up in the elevator. I had a nice corner unit on the fifth floor. I also had a nice bottle of merlot from California I intended on starting on right away, but now that babysitting came up that was out of the question.

Mary's husband had died suddenly almost five years back. She worked three jobs to keep food on the table. I once suggested to her that she could find a cheaper place to live, but she wouldn't hear it.

She and her husband had lived together here for nearly ten years, and she said she couldn't stand to go. It felt too much like leaving her husband behind once and for all. Besides, she hated the thought of pulling the kids out of school.

I admired her, too. She never asked for help, and I didn't think I could do what she did every day. So I offered when I could, taking the kids when she had late shifts. Because what sort of world would it be if no one offered a helping hand?

Sometimes she tried to pay me, but I never let her. It just felt wrong to take money for that sort of thing.

Besides, maybe they'll take my mind off this day! I hoped, going into my condo. I tossed my keys into the bowl beside the door and went to change into something comfier before the kids could get here.

Shower? I wondered. Getting harangued by a billionaire while getting the stink eye from your boss was hard work.

No, I answered myself. Thinking of a shower just made me think of *him* taking his shower earlier while I stood there in his room, waiting.

So instead I settled into the chair by the window that overlooked the corner below. It was Friday night and I was young, but even if I hadn't been babysitting I'd be staying in the whole weekend to work on the material for Ward. Even though I couldn't stand him.

I couldn't stand not doing a good job. *And besides,* I thought, *Mr. Callaghan is the one who has to deal with him in person from now on.* I wouldn't have to see him again.

***

I went into work Monday morning refreshed and ready to go. I felt really good about the work I'd done over the weekend, and every time I remembered that I didn't have to deal personally with Ward again I smiled.

I got to the C&M floor and went for my desk. I'd gotten a nice corner unit as my reward for my last assignment. It wasn't an office, just a cubicle. But it was mine and I'd earned it.

Even if it was right below an air conditioning vent. I compensated for that by not taking off my jacket.

"Hey, Quinn!"

I cringed, trying to hide the expression. *What now?* "Trish," I said, putting a smile on my face.

Trish reminded me of Ward. Pretty and she knew it. And flaunted it. I would say that she probably woke up early to apply all that makeup, but she was usually late.

She always let her bottle-blonde hair down. And she always undid the first half-dozen or so buttons of her blouse. I managed to keep my eyes from straying down to her cleavage.

She also always wore the highest heels she could get away with. Probably to make her ass stick out more. They always gave her a few inches over me, an advantage she pressed at every opportunity.

Coupled with the heels was the skirt. She always wore a skirt, usually one that ended above the knee, despite the normal dress code at C&M leaning more conservatively.

She went over to my desk and picked up the plaque with my name on it, moving it back and forth in her hand so that the bead of light running along it kept dancing between the W and R in my surname.

"So, I heard you screwed up big time with the Ward account." She caught sight of her own reflection on the plaque and paused the movement of it so she could check her makeup in it.

"Did you?" I said. I sat at my desk and leaned back in my chair, stretching my legs out into the kneehole. This earned me a squinty-stare. Trish hated that I got the corner desk. I guess she couldn't find anyone to sleep with who would give it to her.

I basked in her anger. It was a short-lived basking.

Trish dropped my nameplate down onto my desk, grinning when she saw how I winced at the clatter. "Yeah, I did. And if you're not careful, I'll take it away from you. If you haven't already lost it, that is."

I bristled. I worked so hard to get to where I was. Trish was everything I hated in a coworker. She got ahead on her looks alone, chatting up and sleeping with any man higher up the ladder than her.

What was worse was how nice to me she'd been when I first started. I recognized it now as her taking advantage of me. I'd helped her out on a few projects for which she then took all the credit. When I confronted her about it she just winked at me and called me gullible.

She hated me, too, though. Because she knew I got where I was by doing good work.

What made it worse was that I really did think she was quite pretty. Prettier than I was, definitely. I tried not to let the jealousy get to me, but sometimes it did.

"I'm not going to lose it," I replied. I sounded more confident than I felt. Because I remembered the way Mr. Callaghan looked at me at the end of the meeting and I knew Trish might be right.

And I hated the thought that Trish might get a shot at working on the biggest account C&M had taken on since I started working here.

"Really?" Trish said. She grinned, ruby-red lips pulling back to show off a set of perfectly white teeth in a terrible, wolfish grin that made her beauty twist to ugliness.

"Yes, really," I said. I started tapping my foot.

"Hmm…" Trish said. She sat on the corner of my desk. Then she started examining her fingernails. They were long and manicured and the same ruby red as her lips. And I had the sneaking suspicion that they were also fake.

"If you're finished, I have to get to work. You know, that stuff you're supposed to do in exchange for your salary, that stuff?"

Trish smiled, still examining her nails. She started picking at one, cleaning it with another. I clenched my teeth.

"Trish," I said, my jaw tight.

"What? Oh, yes. Your… work," she said, snorting when she looked down at my briefcase.

She seemed to forget that without my "work" all

those months ago she would probably have been out of a job.

Trish stood, rubbing her thumb and forefinger together to grind up whatever she'd found under her nail and then dropping it to the floor. She started walking away, her hips swaying.

I started breathing again, started letting my jaw relax. Then she stopped and spun around, her hair whipping around her face.

"Oh, I almost forgot!" she said.

"Forgot what?" I said. It felt like there was a heavy stone in my stomach. It got heavier when I saw the wolfish grin return to Trish's face.

"Oh, you weren't here when she came down."

"Who, Trish? Who came down?" I said, standing.

She shrugged. "Ms. Spencer's secretary."

"What? Why?" I said, the rock in my stomach turning to an icy block. *What did Trish do this time?*

Seeing my obvious discomfort tickled Trish pink. "Oh, she wanted me to tell you to go see Ms. Spencer as soon as you came in. Apparently she really needs to talk to you."

My eyes wide, I glanced down at the clock on my computer's desktop. It had been 20 minutes since I came into work. I was supposed to get that message straight away. Supposed to have been up there in Ms. Spencer's office fifteen minutes ago at least.

I stared fire at Trish. She lapped it up. "You better hurry. Don't you remember how much Ms. Spencer hates tardiness?"

"Why, Trish?" I asked, feeling like it was pointless to ask but feeling the need to do so anyway.

She shrugged, looking back at me over her shoulder. "I guess it just slipped my mind."

"…Slipped?" I repeated. I stood up too fast, banging my thighs against the top of the desk's kneehole. I sucked in a sharp breath.

I wanted to scream at Trish, but I didn't have the time. I ran for the stairs. Ms. Spencer's office was two floors up. I started up the stairs, taking them two at a time. A pair of men in suits pressed themselves to the wall as I went by. "Sorry!" I called back to them.

I'm going to kill her, I kept thinking, my heart forcing my boiling blood through my veins.

By the time I made it up all the stairs, I could feel my blouse sticking to the small of my back. My pulse pounded past my ears, and the back of my throat felt hot.

This was less from the actual physical exertion of the climbing and more the physical reaction of my body to Trish's antics and my own worry about what Ms. Spencer might say.

I knew I couldn't *actually* kill Trish. Not legally, of course. But even using the term "kill" broadly, I couldn't take her down. She was protected. Mostly by the men she'd used to get to where she was now. They'd put down any complaints of mine to some sort of hand-waving female rivalry or something.

I know because it had happened before. That thing about her taking credit for my work? Yeah, that.

I yanked the door open and found myself on the C&M executive-level floor. Ms. Spencer's office was on the other side.

I walked as quickly as I could, trying to avoid strange looks from the people I passed by. For once, I was grateful for the overpowering air conditioning.

I reached the wood-paneled door to Ms. Spencer's office. It was closed. I paused, taking a moment to compose myself, tugging my jacket down, trying to smooth some of the frizz from my hair.

I took a steadying breath in through my nose and let it out through my mouth. Then I knocked.

"Come in."

I went inside, my pulse pounding so hard I could taste copper in my mouth.

Ms. Spencer looked up the neat pile of papers on her desk. She wore glasses, and she peered up at me over the rims.

I'd always thought the best word to describe her was *striking*. Kind of like Helen Mirren. The streaks of grey in her dark hair, currently tied in a bun similar to mine, lent her authority.

She sighed when she saw me. "Miss Windsor, please have a seat."

Thank God, I thought, sinking into the chair in front of her desk. My knees had just started trembling and I didn't think I could hide it much longer. I pressed my palms together and shoved them between my thighs.

Ms. Spencer considered me, her expression neutral. "In the future, I expect you to be more punctual."

"Y… yes, of course." I didn't try to offer an excuse for my tardiness. I knew that Ms. Spencer didn't like excuses much, for one. For two, I hated giving them.

I was late. Did the reason for my lateness really matter? Besides, giving the real reason would just make me sound like a tattletale. I had the feeling that Ms. Spencer didn't like Trish much, either. But badmouthing your coworkers to your boss didn't feel right to me.

And then she smiled at me. It took me by surprise. "Good, now we can get onto the real business for this meeting. I wanted to tell you myself."

"Tell me what?" I said, leaning forward. My mind kept racing for possibilities, but nothing it touched on made sense.

"The Phoenix Software account is yours. Apparently you really managed to impress Ward."

My mouth opened and my eyebrows knit together. Realizing how ridiculous I looked, I forced my mouth shut until I actually had something to say.

Ms. Spencer had been expecting some positive reaction, so my ambivalence puzzled her. She frowned, a thin line crinkling between her equally thin eyebrows.

"Does that displease you?" she said.

"No, not at all," I said, too quickly, I continued, "It's just unexpected. I thought Mr. Callaghan had decided to handle this account personally?"

Ms. Spencer threaded her fingers together and then planted her elbows on her desk. "You know, I thought the same thing. But Callaghan sent down the order himself. I spoke with him about it. Ward requested you himself. By name. He supposedly followed this request up with the threat that he'd take his account elsewhere when Mr. Callaghan questioned the request."

Why did I have to give him my name? I thought, remembering our conversation in the elevator. I wished so much then that I could have just been another anonymous C&M employee at that meeting.

Ms. Spencer saw the look of panic on my face and offered a warm smile. "Don't worry, I'm certain you're up to the task. From the moment I hired you I knew you'd go far if you applied yourself. And now look, you haven't even made junior partner and you've landed the biggest account this firm has had in a decade at least."

I swallowed heavily, somewhat surprised that I didn't make a cartoonish *gulp* noise as I did.

"I don't know what to say," I said, trying with some success to pull the corners of my mouth into something I hoped resembled a smile of gratitude.

Inside, a flurry of sensations tried tearing me apart.

"Say yes, of course," she replied.

That made me blink in surprise. "You mean I have a choice on the matter?"

That earned me another frown. "Yes, of course you can decline if you like. But I definitely wouldn't recommend it. If you do this and it goes well I can almost guarantee a promotion to junior partner. If you decline... Well, you'll be setting your career back years if I had to guess. And if Ward decides to take his business elsewhere as he has threatened, I don't believe Mr. Callaghan or the other senior partners would like that much."

Now it was Vaughn Ward I wanted to kill. He just made it so I had to choose between my career and my feelings.

And it turned out to be a much harder choice than I thought it would. I'd always considered myself career-oriented. That's why I felt so pleased when Ms. Spencer said that she thought I was going places.

The possibility of promotion to junior partner, probably the youngest junior partner in C&M history was also a tantalizing carrot dangling in front of me.

But then Vaughn Ward's chiseled features appeared in my mind's eye, his lips turning up in that crooked, self-satisfied smile and I suppressed a shiver.

"Do I get any time to think about it?" I said.

"This is a big deal, Miss Windsor. I don't think another opportunity like this will come up again. At least not for a long while… I can see that you're opinionated, that you like to think for yourself. But if you want my unsolicited advice, I would say jump at it. Unless there's a specific reason for your hesitation?"

This was it, I knew. This was my opportunity to tell the woman who was pretty much my mentor at C&M that I hated Vaughn Ward's guts. That the reason I entertained the thought of declining was personal rather than professional.

Ms. Spencer sighed again, "This is something Mr. Callaghan didn't want shared, but he believes that Ward just likes the thought of working with a pretty, young woman. That if you say no now, we're going to offer Ward the chance to work with Trish Matthews." Ms. Spencer's lips twisted when she sat Trish's name, letting me know just what she thought of that proposition.

"You can't be serious," I said, shocked. So shocked that I let my tone slip far more than one might consider professional.

"No. And that's another reason why I believe you

should say yes and show those old men just how talented you are."

I exhaled again, draining my lungs of all the air in them. Then I breathed in slowly, looking out Ms. Spencer's windows at the Boston skyline.

I still couldn't get rid of Vaughn Ward's awful smirk. But I could be professional, couldn't I? I could set aside my feelings for the few months this account would consume and then be rewarded with an incredible promotion.

Junior Partner Quinn Windsor, I kept thinking.

I could stomach him for that long. I knew I could. And besides, some pretty model or actress would catch his attention any time now and he'd just forget about plain little me.

I took another breath and looked back at Ms. Spencer, ready to give her my answer.

Chapter 5

VAUGHN

I'd gotten tired of that hotel suite quickly, so I bought a house in Boston. It was a brownstone in Back Bay. Beautiful and old and full of character.

But what interested me most at the moment was the black-maned beauty sitting across from me in the wingback chair, her bare legs crossed. She wore a dark dress that matched her hair. The hem toed the line between risqué and scandalous, and just looking at those long legs got my heart pumping.

"This is such an incredible house, Vaughn," she said.

We sat near the picture window on the third floor, the sun streaming in. It bathed her already tanned and toned body. We'd met at a party on Saturday night for some modeling agency. They'd heard I was in town and sent the invite over right away.

I didn't mind the attention. Stacey was gone. And I couldn't stop thinking about that Quinn girl from that marketing meeting. I'd needed something to take my mind off things and that something was a lingerie model sitting across from me.

"Yeah, it's nice," I said, "But I have to say right now the only truly beautiful thing I can think about is you."

She blushed. Slowly, so that I got a good look, she let the tip of her tongue trace around her full, glistening lips. Then she leaned forwards in her chair, her cleavage pushing up even higher.

"Is that so?" she said.

For some reason, I kept thinking about the way that Quinn girl blushed when I flirted with her. The way her freckles stood out as her cheeks heated.

This girl across from me was, well, a model. She had

no freckles. Perfect everything. I didn't know what was real and what wasn't in her, and normally I didn't care.

Still, I couldn't help thinking there was nothing unnatural or plastic-surgeon sculpted on Quinn.

"Vaughn?"

"Hmm?" I said, focusing on her again.

"I'd like to do some modeling for you. Would you like that?" she said.

I realized then that I couldn't remember her name. I wanted to say Mandy or Marissa. Something with an M. Normally I was good with that sort of detail. Women liked men who could remember their name.

I leaned back and breathed out, throwing my arms wide across the back of the couch. "Sure, baby."

I got away with it. She smiled and stood up, twisting somewhat to really accent the lines of her body, the curve of her back and the flair of her hips.

She kept her eyes on me the whole time. Reaching back, she unzipped her dress and then stepped out of it.

A few pieces of lacey lingerie hugged her. Sheer brazier, panties so tiny they were more like a couple pieces of string than actual underwear.

Normally such a sight got the blood pumping in all the right places. I did feel something, just not nearly the intensity I was used to.

"Do a little spin for me," I said, swishing one index finger in a circle to illustrate my request.

She sucked her bottom lip into her mouth and let it slip out slowly while she turned around. "Do you like it?"

"Yeah, it's great. Hot," I said, feeling distracted and then feeling annoyed with myself for feeling distracted.

My eyes kept drifting over to the little breakfast bar where my cell sat, my thoughts shifting to wondering when I might hear from C&M about my demands. I'd meant what I said. Quinn or bust.

And not only because I wanted her. In that meeting she'd taken everything I threw at her. I knew what a demanding jerk I could be sometimes, and finding the people who could put up with that and still do good work was harder than it seemed.

"Playing hard to get?" she said.

"Hmm?" I said again, realizing that I'd been looking everywhere but at the beautiful, basically naked lingerie model strutting about in front of me.

Of course, I knew these types of girls were used to getting all the attention they ever wanted from men. It turned them on when you ignored them. Same principle as with cats. Ignore them and they'll come to you.

Except this time I hadn't done it on purpose.

Is that why Quinn is on my mind so much? Because she ignored me?

"I asked if you're playing hard to get," she said. "Because I'm going to tell you now, I always get what I want."

She slunk over to me, her hips swaying in a way that would have normally had me loosening my collar. She sat on my lap and I smelled her perfume. There was something sensual, carnal, and raw about it.

Finally, my body started responding the way I expected it to. I put my hands on her bare thighs and ran them up until I cupped her ass.

"Really?" I said. "Because there's something I should tell you, too."

She leaned in close, grazing my jaw with lips that were soft and warm and inviting, tracing along until she reached my ear. Her hot breaths washed over me, full of promise.

"And what is that?" she said just before taking my earlobe between her teeth and nipping it.

I nuzzled my lips against her neck, in that sensitive spot where it met her jaw, for a moment before replying, "I always get what I want, too."

This is good, I'm hardly thinking about Quinn at all! I thought. Unable to help myself, I glanced over at the phone.

Then she started grinding against me and my breath caught in my throat. "So take what you want," she said.

I made a growling sound in my throat. I picked her up and tossed her down on the couch. Her long legs wrapped around my waist and her fingernails dug into my back, sharp even through my shirt. I hissed. It was a nice pain.

She grabbed the collar of my shirt and yanked my face closer to hers. Her eyes smoldered with desire, and her inner heat flushed her cheeks. "I want you to undress me with your teeth."

I had no problem with that. Still, in the back of my mind this didn't feel as fun and exciting as I knew it should.

Then my cell started blaring, the screen lighting up the wall next to the breakfast bar.

"Hey!" she said.

I didn't even realize what happened until I stood by the breakfast bar with my cell in my hand. At the sound of my phone, I'd disentangled our bodies and left her hot and flushed on the plush couch.

The top three buttons of my shirt were undone, and the ends of my belt dangled in their loops. When had that happened?

The phone vibrated in my hand. "M. Callaghan" the call display read.

C&M, I realized. This was a call to tell me whether they'd accepted my demands or not.

My heart palpitated at the thought of seeing that Quinn and her freckles again.

I hadn't felt this way about someone since... *Since Stacey*, I realized. At that my palpitations disappeared, leaving an almost sick sensation in the pit of my stomach.

"Vaughn? What the hell?"

I answered the call. "What's the news, Callaghan?"

For a second, I heard nothing but Callaghan's breathing. It was something I'd encountered many times in the past. People weren't used to my forwardness.

They wanted their pleasantries and niceties. But those usually just got in the way of the truth.

"Mr. Ward, I wanted to let you know personally that we at C&M are pleased to tell you that we will be continuing our business relationship."

At that, the palpitations and the nerves both returned full force. Then I was the one being quiet. Somewhere inside, I knew that I'd been hoping that they would refuse. It was strange to have my feelings divided in this way. Normally, I was so certain of everything.

It was one of the reasons for my success.

"Mr. Ward?" Callaghan said. His old man's voice sounded even more gravelly over the phone.

"Yes, right. I'm going to want to start right away. I expect I'll need to hold another meeting… Go over things with… with…"

"Miss Windsor?" Callaghan said, "Yes, of course. I'll send everything down the line. We're at your disposal."

"Great," I replied. I hung up. Setting my phone down, I leaned against the breakfast bar. The lacquered wood felt nice and cool against my palms.

"Vaughn?"

My breath caught in surprise. I'd been thinking about where to go from here. I could do that sometimes: get lost in thought. Though it was a habit I thought I'd kicked long ago.

"Yes?" I said. I drummed my fingers on the bar for a second before turning around. She sat on the couch, the seductive lingerie model in her lingerie.

"Are we doing this or what?" she said.

Desire tugged at my insides, but not enough to overcome the inertia of that phone call and what it meant. "No."

She scoffed and stood up, marching over to pick her dress up off the floor. "Whatever happened to that *I always get what I want* talk?"

She pulled her dress up, but in her agitation she couldn't get a good grip on the zipper. I stepped forward and tugged it up for her. She went stiff at my touch, but didn't push me away. I got another whiff of that perfume, but didn't find it as intoxicating as before.

"Sometimes what I want changes. Sometimes I guess even I don't know what I want," I replied.

"Whatever," she replied. She started heading for the stairs.

I watched her, knowing that something inside me was different. And the change happened when I met Quinn.

And it bothered me that the only thing I could compare it to was when I'd met Stacey, who'd left my life so spectacularly.

Chapter 6

QUINN

"Of course he wants to start right away," I said to myself. I'd gotten an email from Mr. Callaghan himself. It was a brief message, but I could read between the lines.

There was a lot riding on this account. Not just the reputation and financial well-being of C&M, but also my career in marketing.

I couldn't help thinking how much nicer, how much easier, this would be if every time I thought about Vaughn Ward my stomach didn't churn. My mind kept returning to that moment in the elevator when he asked what I'd do if he kissed me.

I knew that I should definitely feel offended, maybe a little mortified, as his forwardness. But a part of me I didn't really want to acknowledge found that forwardness attractive and refreshing.

And he is handsome. He was the kind of handsome that would make me ache deep and low if I let it.

I finished loading up a bunch of material, mostly what I'd worked on over the weekend, onto a USB stick and I started the process of turning everything off so that I could go and get this job over with.

Hopefully it would impress Ward, he wouldn't demand any revisions, it would go on to be a successful campaign, and I'd be a junior partner this time next quarter.

Just before I put my computer to sleep a notification came up that I received a new email. I checked it. It was Anne from the art department.

I went over and found Anne seated in front of a bank of flat-screen computer monitors. There had to be half a dozen of them set up on the wall, each one showing a different picture or animation partway to completion.

"Hey," I said, tapping her on the shoulder.

Anne always worked with her headphones on. I could hear what sounded like Katy Perry's latest hit bleeding out from the small speakers. She pulled the headphones down so they rested at her neck and then spun in her chair to face me.

"Quinn! I've got those composites ready that you asked for," she said.

"Great! But why didn't you just email them to me?"

"Because I heard you landed the entire Phoenix Software account. Is it true that *Vaughn Ward* requested you himself?" She grinned up at me.

I always liked Anne. She'd started at C&M a couple months before I did. I'd been fresh out of undergrad and green around the ears and she'd helped me get acclimatized here. We liked to look out for each other.

She was something of a hipster. Curly blonde hair with pink highlights, thick, black-rimmed glasses. She also loved retro skirts.

"How did you know that?" I said, "I don't think anyone's supposed to know that yet but Mr. Callaghan, Ms. Spencer, and me."

She winked. "Let's just say that Callaghan's secretary doesn't mind sharing some office gossip around the water cooler. And why do you look so sour? This is incredible!"

I thought of putting it down to not drinking enough coffee this morning or something, but Anne was right. I should have been ecstatic. And I knew if we switched places I would ask her the same question.

I took a quick look around. The art department was pretty much empty, what with it being close to quitting time.

"It's Ward. I just don't relish the thought of having to work with him."

Anne raised an eyebrow at me, "You make it sound like such a chore to work with the guy *People* rated number

17 in their most beautiful people edition last year."

It was my turn to offer a raised eyebrow. "That's awfully specific. Why do you even know that?"

A hint of rouge touched her cheeks, setting off those highlights in her hair even more. "Can't a girl have fantasies? Ever since I heard C&M had a shot at his account I've been doing my research. But you're trying to distract me. Where's the beef?"

I rolled my eyes. I should have known something was up when she asked me to come see her. I pursed my lips, considering. I decided I might as well tell her. Better than keeping it bottled up.

"I don't like Ward."

"What? Like his company's policies or something? Why not? Did you know he publishes his salary every quarter, and that Phoenix Software is also one of the biggest philanthropic organizations in the country right now?"

I waved at her to stop. She could get a little excited, sometimes. "No, no. Phoenix Software is fine. I don't like Vaughn Ward the man, and I'm not certain I can work with him."

Anne watched me for a little while, considering me like I was a strange animal at the zoo she couldn't quite place. Then her eyebrows lifted. "Are we talking about the same guy? Here, let me pull up a picture…"

She started typing. I leaned down in front of her. "Anne, I know what he looks like."

"Then what problem could you possibly have?"

I sighed. "I've already met him. I was at the preliminary meeting with Mr. Callaghan, who asked me to go check on Ward when he was late. I found him breaking up with his girlfriend. Not ten minutes later, in the elevator ride down, he made a pass at me."

"Vaughn Ward made a pass at *you*?"

Both Anne and I turned and saw Trish standing in the doorway to the art department. She had a manila folder

41

grasped casually in one hand, the sheets inside sticking out at all angles.

Great, I thought. Trish was definitely one of the people who I didn't want to hear what I just said.

I looked at my watch. "It's now officially after five. What are you still doing here?"

Trish hefted the manila folder and gave it a light shake, while also lifting her eyebrows in a *Well, duh?* look. She then came into the office and tossed the folder on a random desk, most of the contents fanning out.

"Vaughn Ward is pretty hot. Way too hot for a little-miss-plain-and-perfect like you," Trish said, giving me a once-over and a shake of her head to accompany the sentiment.

My blood started boiling. Even Anne, normally pretty chill, frowned at the intrusion.

"It doesn't matter how either of us *looks*," I said, feeling self-conscious about what I felt was my too-large nose, and the freckles that never left my face. *Never*. "It's about the job. I just feel that Vaughn won't be professional."

I resisted the schoolyard urge to give my hair a flick, even though it was up in a sensible bun.

Trish might have been somewhat less insufferable if she wasn't so pretty. But that seemed like a moot point to me anyway, since if she wasn't so pretty she probably wouldn't have also been such a bitch.

"Yeah, you keep telling yourself that," Trish said. Then she smiled, putting her finger to her lips as though she just came up with a brilliant idea. "It really doesn't sound like your heart's in this job. I think Ward would be happier with my services. Once Callaghan and Spencer realize that, I'm sure they'll have me take over."

Her eyes glinted with malevolent glee.

An unexpected jealousy jolted me, tightening my throat and making my stomach hot. I knew it shouldn't matter to me that we both knew I wasn't pretty enough for

Vaughn Ward, especially after my little speech there. But it was important.

I took a deep breath, held it, and let it out slowly. This amused Trish, who crossed her arms beneath her breasts and shook her head at me again.

"Trish, I'm going to say this slowly and in small words so that I know you'll understand me," I started. "You will not take this job, or anything else, from me. Ever. I don't care who you sleep with, it's not going to happen."

I wanted to continue from there, to really lay into her, but that edged over from righteous indignation to outright cruelty. Basically, becoming Trish. And that wasn't going to happen ever, either.

The smile dropped from Trish's face, which clouded with anger.

"Whoa, you definitely aren't cute when you're angry," Anne said.

Trish's breath caught, and she sputtered, "You… her… Don't know who you're…"

I took more pleasure than I should have when I shook my head at Trish the same way she did to me.

And Anne also managed another zinger, "Hey, why don't you take a deep breath and count to five before you speak? It works for my niece when she gets flustered. She's in kindergarten."

Trish jabbed her finger at the pile of papers that had spewed from the folder. "You better have those layouts finished by tomorrow morning, or you're fired."

Anne pushed up from her chair, "Hey, you don't have the authority…"

Trish interrupted, "No, I don't. But I'm in good with the people who can. You better remember that. Both of you," she said, shooting us both looks.

She turned to storm out, yanking the door open. Before leaving, she turned back to us again, "And get some new glasses. This isn't 1963." She made sure we saw her

43

roll her eyes before she stepped out, slamming the door behind her.

For a few moments, all I could hear was the gentle hum of the computers. Anne went over and shoved all the papers back into the folder, then came back and plunked down into her chair. "Guess I'll be up all night."

"Hey, I like your glasses. They're cute," I said, my insides switching between compassion for my friend and shock that Trish would say any of that.

"Yeah, it's cool. Still feeling bad about having to work with the 17th most beautiful person in the world?" Anne said, pushing those black-framed glasses back up the bridge of her nose.

"No," I said. It was only a little bit of a lie. I still had misgivings about working with Ward. But now I had one more reason to throw on the *"Do It Anyway"* pile. There was the promotion, the respect, and now the rubbing it in Trish's face aspect to consider.

"What is her problem, anyway?" I said.

It was more a rhetorical question than anything, but Anne nodded like she expected me to ask. "It's jealousy. You're so much better at this than she is, and she can't take it. That, and she thinks she's prettier than you and doesn't know why that's not enough to get ahead. It's kind of sad, when you think about it."

"Sad? Trish?" I said. I'd never put those two concepts together before. Trish always seemed so self-assured.

"Yeah, sad. Don't let her get to you, though. She'll get what's coming eventually… So, when do you start?" Anne asked.

I looked down at my watch again and cringed. "In about 15 minutes. If I can make it to Back Bay that quickly." Not only had Trish trashed what little good mood I had left, she had also made me potentially late.

"Oh! Get your butt in gear, then! Don't worry about me."

I smiled at her and went to the door, pulling it open

when Anne said, "Give him a kiss for me!"

I was glad I was facing away from her so that she couldn't see me cringe at the suggestion. Although part of me bet that Ward was a good kisser. He had such nice lips…

"I hate you," I called back, both of us laughing as the door closed behind me.

***

The GPS on my phone took me to the address I'd been given by Mr. Callaghan's secretary. I stood on the sidewalk in front of the stoop for too long, just looking up at the brownstone that Vaughn Ward had apparently bought on a whim.

It was something of a miracle that I made it in the time that I did, right in the middle of rush hour.

I had to admit that it was somewhat awing that a person could have the kind of money to do that sort of thing.

Of course, it also seemed something like an underhanded insult. He hated the hotel suite I'd had booked for him so much that he literally went and bought a house rather than stay in that room a bit longer.

"Be professional," I told myself. *You don't have to like him. You just have to work with him. Remember, your career is on the line, here!*

I grimaced at that little internal pep-talk and walked up the stoop. When I rang the bell I half expected another hastily-clad model to appear in front of me again.

Instead, Ward answered the door himself. "Quinn!" He seemed taller than I remembered. And the natural light of day on his face warmed his smile, which appeared genuine enough.

"Mr. Ward," I said, trying to ignore the cool rush of excitement in my chest that accompanied my suddenly rapid pulse. *Professional!*

45

"I'm glad things worked out so this could happen," Vaughn said.

Worked out? I thought. He didn't seem to have any clue that because of some whim of his my whole career was on the line. His smile deepened, and my chest fluttered in response.

Stupid Anne, why did she have to tell me that beautiful person thing? Now that I knew that, I could see it. When Vaughn's smile wasn't crooked, both corners of his mouth terminated in the most adorable dimples. His eyes were sharp and clear, and his angular cheeks and chin sported the perfect amount of stubble.

"C&M is happy to accommodate all your needs," I replied, trying to pull this back to nothing but a business interaction.

It helped to think about the trail of broken hearts that littered Ward's wake. Sure, he might be handsome and rich and all that, but he went through relationships like a smoker goes through a pack of cigarettes, burning people up for whatever temporary fix he needed.

We both realized at the same moment that we'd spent at least thirty seconds standing on his stoop, looking at each other.

He scratched at the back of his head and looked up and down the street, which was more brownstones on either side with lots of high-end cars parked along the curb. "Come in. I'll give you the tour."

I stepped inside and my breath caught. It was a beautiful home. Warm wood paneling met a hardwood floor polished to a high, smooth shine. Pieces of modern art accented it all.

It was a great blend of modern styling cues meeting retro-chic. They could do magazine spreads on this place. My brain was already working on a layout and a few choice phrases.

"You like it?" Ward said, watching me take in the space.

And the thing was, it sounded like he really did want my approval. I tried to ignore the flattery of the sentiment, tried reminding myself that we were here because apparently the five-star hotel I'd chosen for him wasn't up to his expectations.

"It's nice. Warm," I said, "Now…" I started meaning to ask if we could get down to work, but then I caught a whiff of it. The unmistakable smell of fresh espresso. And, before I could stop myself, I continued, "Is that coffee?"

It had been something of an exhausting day. Mentally and emotionally, at least. My brain craved caffeine.

"Ah," Ward said, his eyebrows lifting, "I recognize a fellow addict. Come with me."

"Wait, we should…" I started, but Ward wasn't listening. He started down the hall, and before I could help myself I followed. He just had that sort of aura of easy authority around him that following felt right.

We ended up in a kitchen that could also have been on the cover of various home decorating magazines. Granite countertops, an island with a wine cooler in it, skillets hanging down from a rack suspended from the ceiling.

And an espresso machine with enough chrome accents on it to make any hipster red in the face.

Ward went to work quickly, and I heard the hiss of steam and a low buzz as the machine made some fresh-ground espresso.

My mouth started watering. *He makes his own espresso?*

"You know, I had you pegged as an order-everything-in kind of guy," I said, the relaxed and warm atmosphere throwing me off my guard.

I knew that I should tell him to stop. That I didn't want or need his coffee. It stepped over that professional line in the sand that I had drawn.

"Happy to surprise you," Ward replied. "But also somewhat puzzled. I have a pretty wide array of talents. You don't get to be where I am being good at only one thing."

Bravado. Boasting, my mind warned. However, I felt inclined to agree with him. Looking at him now, I saw he wasn't much older than I was. And yet he'd built himself quite the tidy empire.

When he handed me the latte he'd just finished and I took a sip I could feel the surprise spreading on my face. "This is good!"

"Again with the surprise. That wounds me, you know, that you find it so surprising I could be good at something like that."

I took another sip, unable to resist the urge from my caffeine-deprived brain. I perked up right away. Then I sipped again, the scent of the fresh-ground espresso beans filling my sinuses.

When I lowered the cup I saw Ward watching me. "What?" I said, realizing how ridiculous I must look. Suddenly I felt self-conscious. Were there stray hairs coming out of my bun? Did this blouse work well with these pants? Did I have those dark circles under my eyes this morning and if so did I remember to cover them up?

His smile widened. "You have a mustache."

Mortification ran up and down my spine. "Excuse me?"

"From the foam. On your upper lip. What did you think I meant?" Ward replied. "Here, let me."

He grabbed a napkin from a dispenser on the island and started reaching for my face. I recoiled at the last second. "I can do it, thanks."

I had to turn around and face away from him while I dabbed at my mouth. It felt like he had the upper hand so far. I hadn't just crossed that invisible line, I'd rubbed it out of existence.

And I hadn't even shown him any work yet.

Chapter 7

VAUGHN

I leaned back against the countertop, the espresso maker hissing and pinging gently to my left.

Ever since Quinn had arrived, I couldn't stop smiling. I felt like an idiot. Or maybe a kid. But I couldn't stop myself.

I knew that she didn't really like me. In fact, if someone pressed me on the issue, I would say that she'd rather not even be in the same room as me. The same building, even.

I chose to fall back on my cat theory. I wanted her because of the fact that she didn't want me.

I let my eyes run up and down her body. She wore a sensible pantsuit, her hair up in an equally sensible bun, just like before. And just like before, I wanted to know what that hair of hers might look like loose around her shoulders.

She turned around and put her espresso cup on the island a little hard. Some of the liquid splashed onto the granite top. She had trouble dragging her eyes up to meet mine, but she made herself do it.

She definitely had a fire in her. If only she'd let it out.

"Can we get to work please, Mr. Ward?" Quinn said, so desperate to maintain that professional distance.

"Yeah, sure. Show me what you have," I said. I kept looking at those freckles on her cheeks. I saw the way she tried covering them up.

And then those cheeks of hers started to flush and I realized I was staring. However, I couldn't tell at first whether it was a flush of embarrassment or anger.

"We'll need a computer," she said, trying to prompt me to some action.

I took her up to the second level where I had a study set up. As with the rest of the house, it was one of those blended classic and modern areas. Warm wooden bookcases, huge desk with an overstuffed chair in the kneehole, that sort of thing.

"This is nice," Quinn said, standing in the doorway, "But where's the computer?"

I stood behind her, looking into the room over her head. I caught the barest hint of some fresh, clean scent and knew it was her. I had the urge to wrap my arms around her, clasp my hands just below her navel, and pull her back against me so that I could nuzzle my lips against her neck, right where it met her shoulder.

"Oh, it's in here," I said. I put my hand on her shoulder, intending on asking her to let me go past. She stiffened at my touch and I withdrew.

Before I could say anything she turned around and looked up at me. This time I knew that red flush in her cheeks was anger. At me.

"*Mr.* Ward," she said, stressing that title so as to maintain her professional distance, "This is nothing but business to me. It will never be anything other than business. I'm good at my job, and I'm sure if you put aside whatever this is, you'll see that. Do you understand?"

I struggled to refrain from making some remark about how good she looked when she was angry. Really, I did. It wasn't natural for me to not speak my mind.

However, I also got the sense that she was, in some way, expecting me to say something like that.

So I leaned against the door frame, thumbs hooked in my pockets, and nodded. "I know you're good at your job. Why? What other reason could I possibly have for demanding that you be the one to handle my account?"

That put a damper on her righteous indignation. I watched her try and rally her anger again and fail. She frowned once, then again, unprepared for that remark.

"Well…" she started, "It's because the last time you

and I were together you said you wanted to kiss me…"

"Oh, that, right. I'm thinking more of how you handled yourself in that meeting. Answering all my questions, not being scared of me. Callaghan's just a yes man. Trust me, I know them when I see them. You're not one."

She cocked an eyebrow at me, her defenses still up but not at full power. "I'm not a man, for one."

At last, some humor! I thought. There was a tiny sparkle in her eyes. It was that fire inside I'd noticed earlier. That heat that wanted to escape if only it got the chance. A tingle of excitement ran down the front of my stomach.

"Definitely not," I said, smiling at her. It was a good smile, I knew. It had been on magazine covers. I knew exactly what effect it had on women.

The heat came back to her cheeks and she dropped her eyes from mine.

Ah, there we go. I figured I had her. Beautiful brownstone, good coffee, the general warmth of the room, some charm and some flirting. The perfect recipe to loosen her up.

"Are you finished?" she asked, and I saw that the warmth in her cheeks wasn't from my skillful flirting but rather another shot of anger directed at me.

I unhooked my thumbs from my pockets and held my hands up in surrender, "Yes."

She narrowed her eyes at me, wondering whether this was another joke or if I was serious. The thing was, I wasn't certain of the matter myself.

It would certainly be easier to call it a day with her. I had another invite to some high profile movie junket tonight. Plenty of starlets would be there.

Except I found I liked the challenge. No woman had challenged me like this since college, and it got my blood pumping with the unexpected thrill of it.

So I brushed past her, inhaling her scent again as I went. It made me throb deep inside.

"So, about that computer?" Quinn said. She reached into her pocket and pulled out a jump drive.

"You didn't say the magic word," I said.

Her face brightened again and I loved it. It also surprised me how she otherwise managed to maintain her cool.

"May I please use your computer?"

I touched a hidden button on the desk and the computer monitor folded up out of the top, right above the kneehole. It was one of those composite things with the USB jacks and all that built into it.

When the screen finished folding out, a minimalistic keyboard and a touchpad also came up. I pulled the overstuffed leather chair out and offered it to her.

She squinted at me again, once more questioning the purity of my motivations. I took my hands off the chair and stepped away. She sat down and went to work, plugging the jump drive in and browsing through the files.

"I spent the weekend thinking about the upcoming release of your latest app. The art's just a mockup for now. But I think this is just the thing you need. This is a still that will run in all the major software publications: *Wired, PCWorld,* and the like."

I leaned over, putting one hand on the top of the chair for support. I had to squint a little to read it, some of the text was small on the screen. It took me a second to feel her eyes on me.

"That's good!" I said. And it was. The colors were eye catching, the tag line grin-inducing. Funny and witty. Just the sort of thing I wanted.

From the corner of my eye, I saw Quinn's shoulders sag with relief. Then she launched in the other material, telling me where she got her ideas from. What made her think of certain things.

I could see the passion she had for her work, and how much of herself she put into it. And I have to say, that was a turn-on for me. I liked people who knew what they wanted and how to make it happen.

She loved the challenge of it, and took joy in creating.

After perhaps a couple minutes I couldn't keep my sight on the screen anymore. I just couldn't stop myself from watching how animated she became. The way she smiled and the way that smile made a dimple in one cheek but not the other.

Definitely the girl next door, I thought. The kind of girl who was so damn hot without even knowing it, without even trying it. Hell, it looked to me like Quinn actively tried to dull her looks down.

"So, what do you think?" she said, finishing a PowerPoint slideshow about the proposed rollout schedule and distribution of the various ads. "I know it's all a little rough, but, well, I wasn't exactly expecting to be the one doing all this…"

"It's great," I said, "I love it all."

My heart lurched in my chest when she smiled at me. It was an unreserved moment of joy. She knew she'd done a good job and she'd been afraid I wouldn't like it.

When she realized what she was doing, she dropped the smile and turned back to the monitor. "Like I said, it's preliminary. Rough. But it will be finished by the window you specified."

I patted the top of the chair and turned away. I perused the spines of all the old books on the shelves, running my finger along them. I stopped at one and tapped it. Then I pulled it off and leafed idly through the pages.

It was *Pride and Prejudice*. A first edition, I knew. They were all firsts in here. "You know, you're not my usual type," I said, closing it up. I pushed it back into its spot.

"I hope I'm not your unusual type, either," she said. She pushed the chair back and stood, pulling the jump drive from the computer as she went. The final PowerPoint slide disappeared from the screen.

"And I'm going to take this as approval to continue

with what I've showed you. In the future, I think we should correspond through email. I can show you everything just as easily."

In two steps I stood in front of her. She swallowed, but didn't back down. "You know what? I think that you like me. I think that you want me and it scares you."

"I could never..." she said, dropping her eyes, lowering her chin towards her chest.

I placed my hand against her cheek, my pinky finger pressed lightly against the bottom of her jaw, and lifted her face so that she looked at me again. "Just give in. I promise you'll like it."

Then I tried to kiss her. Her eyes started closing, her lips started parting. They trembled a little and I knew that somewhere she did want me. My heart sang in my chest, my blood suddenly boiling in my veins.

It felt right. It felt more intense than anything I'd felt for a woman in a long time. *Since I first met Stacey*, I thought, and all the ones before her that were like her.

It gave me pause. A pause long enough for Quinn to snap herself from her own spell. She grabbed my wrist and tore my hand from her cheek.

"I hate men like you. You think that because you're so hot and so successful that no woman could possibly resist you. Don't you remember what I said when we came in here? It's not going to happen. Never."

She turned to go, to storm out. I knew I couldn't let her, not now. She got to the door.

"Quinn, wait. Please," I said.

And by some miracle she stopped in the doorway. It was the professional in her, I knew. The part of her that insisted she do a good job at everything.

Although it didn't surprise me too much. I wasn't stupid. I knew this sort of job could make or break her whole career. I knew she had a lot riding on this. I just needed her to stay a little longer, and I needed to use the tools I had available.

"Yes?" she said, looking back at me but not leaving the doorway.

"Stay a bit longer."

"I shouldn't," she said, "It wouldn't be professional of me."

"I won't tell your boss if you don't," I shot back. "A few minutes is all I ask."

She shrugged and shook her head, giving in. I brushed past her and led her upstairs to the third floor with its large living room and great view. I could see her admiring the place.

"This is really nice," she said. She ran her hand along the breakfast bar and stopped to admire a piece of abstract art I had on the wall. Then she went over to the windows and looked out onto the street.

She nodded. "Yup. Nice. Mr. Ward, I'm happy you like my work so far, but I really think I should go now."

I leaned against the banister, not blocking her way, but not inviting her to go, either.

"You should? Why? Are you afraid something might happen if you don't?"

"No," she said, getting that determined look on her face again. But now I knew that somewhere inside she did want me. She felt that draw other women felt around me. She was just better at resisting it.

Whoever thought that could be such a turn-on?

"So stay, then. Prove yourself right," I said. I pushed away from the banister, moving so that I stood closer to her.

"No promotion is worth this," she said, almost under her breath. I still made it out. "I'll show myself out. Thanks for the coffee."

She started for the stairs, but before she got there I spoke again. "Wait, just one more thing."

Before she could ask what I reached out and plucked at the pins holding her bun in place. She let out a startled gasp as her hair tumbled in waves to her shoulders.

Having it in a bun all day like that made the ends curl up just so. It framed her face, making her look more feminine. The fair hair bringing those dark freckles out even more.

The throb inside of me turned into an ache.

"Hey!" she said.

"Just like I thought," I said. "You're beautiful, Quinn." I offered her the bobby pins. I had to take a deep breath to steady myself. I found her intoxicating. I had to have her.

Chapter 8

QUINN

He held the bobby pins out to me. The ends of my hair brushed against my ears and tickled at my neck.

I didn't know how to feel. Mortification kept trying to well up from the pit of my stomach. But the way he kept looking at me stirred heat within me instead. I couldn't deny that I was attracted to Ward. That I wanted him.

But I knew that I shouldn't. He was exactly not my type. He would be so bad for me, and I wouldn't exactly be good for him, either.

The woman inside me still yearned for him, though.

And his words still echoed in my head. *You're beautiful.* And that's how I knew it was all some game, because I wasn't.

"No," I said, taking the bobby pins back and squeezing them in my palm. "I'm not."

I had to admit that it was even nicer up on this floor then on the first two. The couches, the art, the window, it all encouraged me to stay awhile.

When I first came up, though, I caught the hint of something. Some expensive perfume that just dripped sex. He'd had another woman up here not so long ago. Other women, plural, probably. They threw themselves at him and he was always there catch them.

I wished he'd just let me slip on by.

Smelling that had made me want to go, made me remember who he really was. But why did he keep looking at me that way?

"I think that you've been around me enough to know that I don't pull my punches," Vaughn said. "And you, Quinn, *are* beautiful. I noticed that the first time I saw you."

He closed the distance between us so that I saw almost nothing but his face looking down into mine. I couldn't stop my body from responding to the proximity. My heart thumped, my mouth went dry. A warm tingle ran down through me.

"No, I'm not," I repeated, shaking my head.

He didn't say anything else. He put his hand to my cheek again, steadying my head so that I couldn't contradict him by shaking it anymore.

This time when his face descended closer to mine I didn't stop it. I parted my lips to deny him again, but before I could he fitted his mouth against mine.

The first thing I felt was the prickle of his stubble against my skin. Then electricity filled and suffused me, from my scalp to my toes.

I remembered thinking, *He really* **is** *a good kisser.* His mouth was warm on mine. His lips gentle yet insistent. My eyes drooped closed before I could stop them, and my calves tensed, trying to lift me higher so that he might kiss me more easily.

His other hand, the one that didn't cup my cheek, slid down my waist, coming to rest on the swell of my hip. He squeezed, then pulled me against him.

My insides turned to warm jelly. I could feel the power in him. He was like a magnet I couldn't resist, drawing me inexorably towards him.

Then he stopped. And I didn't want him to stop. He pulled back a bit, his face still filling my vision, his hands still on my cheek and my hip, his eyes fixed on mine. I could still feel the prickle of his stubble. I could feel my heartbeat in my lips.

I licked my lips. I wanted to look away from him, but I couldn't. It was that magnetism.

"See?" he said, stroking the soft and delicate skin

below my eye gently with the ball of his thumb.

My instinctual desires flared up again, and I could see. I could see myself letting go of my resistance, pushing him down onto that couch back there, the two of us tearing at each other's clothes until there was nothing between our naked bodies.

I parted my lips to reply, but couldn't find the words. I couldn't decide what I wanted to say. Whether I wanted to tell him to kiss me again or to take his hands off me.

Ward's eyes followed the movements of my lips, his jaw working. He swallowed heavily and I knew he wanted to kiss me again. His eyes moved to my hair, taking in the way it waved, the way the ends curled a little.

Then he pushed his fingers into my hair, threading them through my locks. He squeezed just enough to make me gasp, to make me throb inside.

"I'm going to kiss you again," he said, his voice throaty and low. His fingers squeezed a little tighter in my hair, his other hand pulling me a little harder against his body.

He pursed his lips, wetting them. And then he came in for the kill. My heart palpitated again, leaving me hot and trembling all over.

My cell started chiming in my pocket. He tried ignoring it, but the sudden sound broke whatever charm or spell he had cast on me. I put my hands between our bodies and pushed.

His fingers slipped from my hair and he stumbled back a step before catching his balance.

I tugged my blouse straight, and then I turned away from him and pulled my cell out. I frowned at the phone then thumbed the answer button across the screen.

"Mary? What's up?" I said.

"Oh, Quinn, I'm so happy I caught you. I wanted to catch you before you got home tonight but I haven't seen you come in. Look, I'm really sorry, and this is such short notice, but can you watch the kids again tonight? I'm so sorry, but I really need to take this shift and it's so last minute…"

I started cooling on the inside, the fog around my mind lifting. The fantasies of our two bodies pressed together on the couch receded. It felt good, like a return to normal. This was a problem I could solve, unlike the problem Vaughn Ward.

That problem twisted and changed every time I thought I had a handle on it.

"It's okay, Mary. I'm over in Back Bay right now, but I'll start home right away. I'll be as fast as I can. And it's not a problem. Not at all."

Mary's relief was palpable over the phone, the tension and worry leaving her voice. "You're a lifesaver, really. And please, let me pay you this time."

"How about you just send a few boxes of mac & cheese up with them and we'll call it even? I have to replenish my stores."

I should be paying you, I wanted to say. She had no idea what sort of trouble she had just gotten me out of. The least I could do was look after Alex and Charlie for the night.

I could feel Vaughn standing behind me, feel his eyes on me. His confusion, like Mary's relief, was palpable. And like Mary's relief, I enjoyed it. "Just send them on up right now if you like. Alex knows where I keep my spare key. I'm sure they'll be fine until I get there."

Mary continued thanking me until I told her she shouldn't waste any more time talking to me. I ended the call and slipped the phone back into my pocket.

"Did you enjoy that?" I asked him.

"Yes. Didn't you?"

I didn't answer his question. "Good. Because it's never happening again."

"Is there a problem?" Vaughn said. The concern in his voice sounded real, surprisingly. I had to give it to him, he was good at what he did.

And he's a damn good kisser, too! My lips still tingled. I wasn't about to admit that, though.

"Nothing that can't be solved with a box of mac & cheese," I said. "And now I really am going. As far as I'm concerned, none of this ever happened." I walked down the stairs, watching my hand slide along the banister.

Chapter 9

VAUGHN

I could still taste Quinn on my lips while I watched her walk down the stairs and disappear.

I thought about calling out to her, but knew that I shouldn't. She liked doing the opposite of what I said, and asking her come to back now would just push her further away.

I rubbed my bottom lip with the tip of my finger, pulling my thoughts back to what it felt like to kiss her. I thought I'd gotten just a touch of that heat inside her, and it burned me.

My head was all sorts of messed up. A flurry of thoughts and desires blew through my mind, and all I could do was go sink into the wingback chair closest to the window.

I hadn't really caught much of her phone conversation. I gathered someone had asked her for help and she jumped at the chance. Probably because she knew that I had her dead to rights. I had sensed that desire inside her, that need to move things up to the next level.

And now that she had denied me again, it made me want her even more.

I tried not to think about how it worried me that she made me feel the way she did. How every other time I'd felt that way about someone it never worked out. How I always managed to sabotage myself.

I smiled at the irony. I was rich and successful. A few magazines even thought I was handsome. And in spite of all that there was still something inside of me that was broken. Something that so many other people without my circumstances had.

And what was that about mac & cheese? I couldn't figure

Quinn out, not completely, and I knew that made up good portion of my attraction to her. One of the things that drew me to her.

And I thought that maybe she experienced something similar with me, but that it was also one of the big reasons that made her push me away even in the middle of a kiss.

Maybe someone hurt her in the past? Someone that I reminded her of? I wondered.

It was all too much to think about. Especially right now, what with my new app launch coming up. If anything, I should have all my efforts focused on that. I couldn't, though.

Maybe I just need to get her out of my head, I figured. That hadn't gone so well earlier with that lingerie model earlier, but I could give it another try. There was that movie junket tonight.

Starlets and alcohol. The perfect way to get your mind off anything.

I grabbed my phone to find the details.

Chapter 10

QUINN

I got back to my condo and found Alex and Charlie sitting on the floor between the couch and the TV, a *SpongeBob* episode playing on the screen.

"Hey, guys," I said, feeling exhausted. It was like that kiss had burned me up on the inside, and I couldn't stop thinking about it, or him.

Is he thinking the same thing? I wondered, followed by, *It doesn't matter what he's thinking about.*

"Quinn!" the kids said, getting up when they saw me.

They stopped short, looking at me funny.

"What is it? Did I grow a second head?" I said.

They giggled. Then Alex took the lead, "You look pretty, Quinn. Like a girl."

I put my hands on my hips. "Well, I am a girl. And are you saying I don't look pretty normally? Because if you are, then you're in for the tickling of a lifetime."

"No!" Charlie said, laughing, "It's your hair. It's long. And pretty. What did you do to it?" She tugged at her own hair, which her mom kept trimmed to just below her chin. I recognized that look. I'd given it to older girls myself. That mix of awe and jealousy.

"Was it for a boy?" Alex broke in. He wrinkled his face at the thought. At his age, girls were still just cootie factories I suppose.

I looked down and saw my hair resting on my shoulders, still wavy, still a little curly at the end.

"That's none of your business," I said, winking at them. I felt self-conscious, so I excused myself and went to the bathroom.

I leaned over the vanity and looked at myself in the mirror. I guess my hair looked okay. But what was Ward playing at? I still had that nose. And those freckles. Big, soft eyes with eyebrows that always seemed too thick no matter how often I plucked at them.

Then I shoved my hand into my pocket and felt the bobby pins. The ones he'd pulled out and then offered to me.

I didn't put them back in, but I did grab a hair elastic from the drawer on the left and used it to pull my hair into a ponytail.

I grabbed the pins from the vanity and looked at them against the pink skin of my palm. *What happened back there? What came over me?*

Whatever it was, it had been a mistake. Something I couldn't and wouldn't let happen again. I tried to be an adult about it. I had to admit to myself that I found him physically attractive. There wasn't anything wrong about that.

It was giving into that attraction that I shouldn't let happen.

But I had experience with men who knew they were handsome and knew that women liked them. Experiences and pains I didn't feel like reliving. I wanted to concentrate on my future, on my career, and on myself.

I'll make sure we do everything over the phone or email. The easiest way to get rid of temptation was to get rid of the object of that temptation. Ward and I had had our face-to-face meeting and that should be enough to satisfy the higher-ups back at the C&M.

I hoped.

"Quinn! Can we have something to eat?" Charlie called. I squeezed the bobby pins. I still felt confused. Nothing was resolved yet.

"Yeah, I'll make something in a minute!" I called back. I liked having the kids here. They were a distraction, of course. But they also made me feel good. But eventually their mother would want them back. I wondered if maybe I should buy a cat.

I opened my fist and looked again at the pins. *It was a kiss, nothing more.* And it wouldn't happen again. Ward was probably busy with another model by now anyway. Someone more suited to him. Basically, someone who was the opposite of me.

I pushed down on the pedal for the little metal trashcan I kept in the bathroom and tilted my palm over it until the pins fell down into the plastic bag.

***

I was cautiously optimistic when I sat down at my desk the next day. Trish wasn't there to badger me. There weren't any intimidating emails from anyone with the ability to fire me.

And also nothing from Vaughn Ward. No news was good news, right? I congratulated myself, figuring that I got to him.

Now I could concentrate on the work. Last night while getting the kids ready for bed (I let them use my bed and I took the couch) I'd had an idea. I brought up one of the magazine stills.

Then Anne showed up. "Hey!" She gave me an expectant smile.

"Hi," I said.

"So…?" Anne said, looking around my cubicle. She ran one finger along the false wall, tracing over my calendar as she walked around my desk to see what I was doing.

"I'm trying to think if I should change the wording a little," I said.

Anne leaned over my chair and squinted at the ad. She nodded approvingly at the layout, which was her work.

"You know what? I don't think you've ever been interested in more than the artwork before. What are you looking for?" I asked.

"You had another meeting with Vaughn Ward last

night…"

"Yeah?"

"Just the two of you, alone in his house. Vaughn Ward, the 17th sexiest person alive, and you, alone."

Yeah, and I can still feel the prickle of his stubble on my lips, I thought, but I wasn't going to tell her that. "So, what?"

"So, *details*, of course! Come on, you can kiss and tell with me!" Anne said, grabbing the back of my chair and giving it a little bit of a shake.

"Who said anything about kissing?" I said, my throat tightening. "It was a business meeting. A consultation."

Anne went still behind me. I could sense the inner workings of her mind, trying to figure out what my tone meant. "Was there kissing?"

"There was coffee. He made me coffee. A latte, actually," I said. It had been a good one, too. I thought about how I'd remarked to him how surprised I was he could do that sort of thing himself. And then how he said he liked surprising me.

"He made it himself? Like with his own hands?"

"Yes, Anne, he ground the beans between his fists and used his own inherent hotness to steam the milk."

"You know what I mean!" she said, giving my shoulder a playful swat. We both laughed. I knew I should tell her that I needed to work (because I wanted this over with as quickly as possible) but it felt good to gab a bit.

"Yeah, sorry. Yes, he made it himself, he didn't order it or anything. I just can't figure him out," I said, turning a bit in my chair so that I didn't have to crane my neck all the way around to look at her.

"Do you want him to kiss you?" Anne asked.

"What sort of question is that?"

"An honest one."

"No," I said. "I don't. He's just another flirt who thinks he can get any woman he wants. He just happens to be incredibly wealthy and handsome, too."

"Is he ever!" Anne started gushing. She actually

clasped her hands to her chest. She walked back around to the front of my desk and stared dreamily up at the tiles in the drop ceiling, as though Ward's angelic face might deign to look down on her.

"Have you been doing more *research* on him?" I said, wondering how much time she'd spent last night going through gossip sites and Google image searches.

"So much research!" she said, unabashed. "That man is so hot! I'd eat him up. Every last bite. And then I'd ask for seconds."

"You're adorable," I said, smiling. Although there was also this tiny flair of some feeling inside my chest. It took me a second to recognize it. Jealousy. The kind that made me want to tell Anne to knock it off.

"If it were me instead of you last night, oh, Quinn, you don't even want me to get started…"

"Get started on what?"

We both jerked at the unexpected interruption. Vaughn Ward stood beside my corner cubicle, one arm resting casually along the top of the false wall. He wore a nice grey blazer with a white shirt on underneath. No tie. The top button was undone.

When Anne saw who it was, she actually said, "*Eep!*" her eyes going wide and her cheeks warming up enough to glow.

"Mr. Ward!" I said, standing up. I felt the immediate need to tidy my desk, even though it was already pretty clean. I also felt the need to reach up and touch my hair to make sure my bun was still in place. I resisted both urges.

"Quinn," he said, then he turned his eyes to Anne, "…and Quinn's friend."

Even under the harsh and unforgiving fluorescent lights of the office Ward looked good. That definitely wasn't fair.

My heart started pounding again. *Yes*, I thought, *he's good looking. It's okay to think that. Just don't act on it.* But my body wanted to act on it so badly. I put it all down to

69

physical desire.

Poor Anne looked like she might melt into a puddle if something didn't happen soon.

Ward had given Anne a cursory glance, but all his attention was now on me. The beginnings of one of his crooked smiles tugged at one corner of his mouth.

Probably thinking about that kiss last night. What a huge mistake that was! Except I couldn't help thinking about that kiss, too.

"Mr. Ward," I started again. "What are you doing here?"

"I was doing some thinking last night, and I thought that we need to have more of these meetings. Email's such a poor substitute for face-to-face interaction. Don't you agree?" Ward said, addressing his question to Anne.

"Uh, yeah. Face-to-face," Anne said. I don't think she had blinked since Ward showed up.

Knew it, I thought, *there was no way I was getting off that easy.*

I gave him a polite smile. "Perhaps you're right. However, right now I'm actually in the middle of something and I don't really have the time…"

He shook his head, "Oh, not right now. I was thinking tonight. You found my place once, I'm sure you can do it again. And *no* is unacceptable."

I bristled. What sort of bravado was this? Didn't he know I wasn't interested? Hadn't I made that clear?

Except I knew that I hadn't. I'd said one thing and done another. Told him I had no interest in him and then folded like a pair of deuces when he kissed me.

I didn't want to answer him right away, and I saw an out in Anne. "Mr. Ward, you liked the layouts and the artwork in those roughs I showed you, right?"

He nodded. "They were great. Just what I was looking for."

I smiled again, then motioned to Anne. "This is Anne. Anne Snyder. She did those layouts. I think Anne already knows who you are."

"Excellent work, Miss Snyder," Ward said, offering her his hand. She looked down at it, her eyes wide enough that I could see the whites.

The thing that really got to me was how casually Ward acted. He saw nothing strange in Anne's behavior around him. To him, I figured, it must be normal. This was just how women acted around him.

She put her trembling hand in his and he gave it two pumps.

I crossed my arms, feeling somewhat more immune to his charms. Although that little spark of jealous refused to be extinguished.

"Anne, don't you have those new layouts you need to finish?" I said.

"...Layouts?" Anne said, the English language failing her.

"Yes, layouts. Artwork. Those things you like creating so much? Shouldn't you get back to them?"

"Yes. Work. Artwork," Anne said. With some hesitation she walked away. I wondered if maybe she just went around a corner and watched us from there. So long as she was too far away to hear anything we said I didn't care.

Good, she's gone. I thought. But then something else occurred to me. It was unusual for Anne to come to my desk. It wasn't so strange to see Trish wandering around, avoiding work.

Trish, who wanted to steal this account from me. Trish, who was hotter than me and willing to use that fact to get ahead.

I took a look around, but didn't spot her. That didn't mean anything, though. She could appear whenever she wanted. I had to get Ward out of here before that happened.

"Is there a problem?" Ward asked.

I lowered my voice. My heart pounded in my ears.

"Yes, there's a problem. You shouldn't be here."

"I've hired your firm to handle advertising for me. You are the person at this firm in charge of my account. There's no reason for me to not be here. Besides, maybe I just wanted to see you again."

"I told you already that that's not a good idea. For either of us. I don't want this," I said. I put my hands on my desk and leaned closer to him to make sure he could hear me, to make sure he could see I meant it.

"No. I don't believe that and I don't think you do, either. What are you so afraid of?"

That spark of jealousy in my chest burst into a sudden gout of hot anger. "I'm not afraid of anything. Especially not you..." I caught something out of the corner of my eye. I thought it was Trish at first, but it wasn't. "What's it going to take to get you out of here so that I can do my job?"

"It's going to take you admitting that we have something here, between us. And you coming by my place again tonight."

My kneejerk reaction was to tell him there was nothing between us, and for him to get out of here before I called security. Except that there was something between us, even though I resisted it.

And besides, I figured this time I'd be ready. No getting disarmed by his charm again.

Then I heard Trish's voice. I could pick it out of the general clamor of the office by its *me, me, me* tone. And it sounded like she was headed this way.

"Fine," I said.

"I knew it," he replied.

Trish laughed at something, the sound grating down my spine. And she was definitely closer than before. I didn't know what her reaction to seeing Ward might be, only that I wouldn't like it.

Strangely, I was less worried about her trying to steal the account and more about what effects her inescapable flirting might have on him.

"Can I get back to work?" I said, giving my monitor a pointed look.

"I look forward to seeing what you've come up with later." He looked at me, and I realized that he was admiring me again.

I couldn't help the heat that rushed to my cheeks. The heat that made those freckles I hated stand out even more than they already did.

Before I could ask him to go again, he broke off the look and walked away.

Trish came around the corner then. She stopped when she saw me standing rather than sitting at my desk. She followed my line of sight, catching Ward's back before he disappeared around the bend to get to the elevators.

"Who was that?" she said.

"Who?" I said. I was distracted with trying to control myself.

She sneered, "The hot guy who you were staring at."

"Him? I... uh... A new intern, I think. And I wasn't staring!" I said, miffed at her accusation.

She wore a tight blazer that pressed her cleavage together and her perfume followed her around in a cloud.

She sniffed. "Don't play that game with me. You had those big, hungry puppy dog eyes. A little desperate, if you ask me."

"I wasn't asking you. And I wasn't staring," I said, forcing my legs to unlock so that I could sit down. I was relieved far more than I should have been that she hadn't seen Ward. But now I wanted her to leave.

She leaned against my cubicle at the same spot where Ward had been moments earlier. She looked down the hall where he went.

"Well, what I saw of the back looked pretty good. Tell me, sweetie, is the front of the same caliber?"

I shrugged, staring pointedly at my monitor.

"If it is, I look forward to seeing this intern around

more often. I think there's a few things I could get him to help me with."

I knew she was just trying to get a rise out of me. I didn't have to look at her to know that she smirked at me.

"It's a free country," I said, "Now, do you mind?"

Trish shook her head and then strutted away. I didn't know if she did mind, but I knew that I did.

Chapter 11

VAUGHN

I had wondered if Quinn might leave her hair down. She had put it up, though. I walked out to my car, parked on the street.

I couldn't shake the image of her standing in the third floor of my brownstone with her hair free around her shoulders.

I sat down and cranked the engine, the Audi firing up with a satisfying purr.

It was a nice car. The kind of car people expected someone like me to drive, so I did. I did a lot of things because I figured people expected them of me.

Part of me wondered if I should just leave well enough alone. I recognized how close this felt to the other times a woman caught my interest. And by that I meant caught it for more than a one night go.

They always started the same. This intense, almost inexplicable attraction. From there it varied. The relationship could last just a few weeks, or even months. I guess it depended on how long it took things to get serious.

And when they got serious I got out. And I was usually the one to end it, either by action (like telling Stacey it was nice when she said she loved me) or otherwise.

A woman in a grey Camry honked at me and flashed her lights. She wanted the spot. I waved at her and pulled away from the curb.

"She's different, though," I said. Quinn was different. None of the other women I'd felt like this about had held out like this. In fact, most of them started like that cute Anne girl Quinn worked with.

Does that mean that maybe things might work out differently?

I wondered, turning the volume down on the stereo to stop whatever mindless radio chatter spat out at me from the speakers.

Because, to tell the truth, I was getting tired of myself. I used the women to try and escape for however long I could. Whether it was just a single night, a weekend on the French Riviera, or for the few months it took for the papers to start to speculate about my true relationship status. However long it could last, I used them.

My cell started ringing so I thumbed the button on my steering wheel to answer it. Bluetooth had to be one of my favorite things, right after a beautiful body.

"Vaughn?"

"That's me. Who is this?"

"You mean you don't remember?" the woman said, she sounded miffed. I had to admit, her voice did seem familiar, and she did have my number.

"Jog my memory," I said, coming up to a stop light a bit fast. I hit the breaks and the car halted almost right away.

"We met at that movie party…" she started.

I cut her off, "Oh yeah. Jasmine, right?" I remembered her now. She was an up-and-comer in Hollywood. The party was for some big, special-effects laden blockbuster. You know the kind. The one you watch once at the theater, are entertained by, and then can't remember a week later?

Jasmine and I had hit it off at the bar right away. And from there it ended where it always did, with her in my bed. Though I wasn't quite sure why I'd given her my number.

Come to think of it, that popcorn movie thing worked pretty well as a metaphor for my night with Jasmine. It had been good while it was happening, but now it faded away into the background with all the others.

She had been my attempt to put Quinn out of my mind. Because I knew if I could stop it now, it would save us both a lot of trouble. However, I have to say I thought more about what it might have been like to spend the night with Quinn.

And that just made me want her more.

"Are you free tonight?" Jasmine said, "There's another party I know about. And I have a friend or two coming that I think would love to meet you. And they'd be down for *anything*."

"Sorry, I've got plans," I said.

"What?" Jasmine said, surprised. I was a bit surprised, myself. That wasn't the type of thing I usually turned down.

"It was fun, Jasmine. But do me a favor and delete this number from your phone."

"I knew you were an asshole," she said, her shock turning to anger. She ended the call.

It wasn't the first time a woman had called me that, or something like that. Not even the first time they'd said they'd known all along. Yet she, and all the others, had gone along with it anyway.

I knew they found something hot and arousing about that. They liked a man who didn't give a damn, a man who'd use them and lose them. Because the thing was, they were using me, too. It was one of those vicious cycles.

I decided to put an end to that while I was in Boston. No more random hookups, no matter how much I wanted it, or how much they wanted it. Because I knew they wouldn't satisfy like they used to.

I knew Quinn was the sort of girl who didn't like that. I knew that was one of the reasons she resisted her attraction to me; she knew what kind of guy I was. I wasn't good enough for her and we both knew it.

And I wanted to be.

So when I pulled up in front of my brownstone, I deleted Jasmine's number from my phone, as well as several texts and emails telling me about various parties and get-togethers where I might fall into another trap.

I thumbed the button on my fob and the Audi chirped behind me. *Now, how to spend the rest of the day?* It wasn't even lunch yet, and Quinn wouldn't be over for hours.

Maybe a nice dinner? I thought. I enjoyed cooking, and Quinn had been surprised when I did something easy like use a machine to make her a latte. What would she do if she found I could do up some chicken cordon bleu, or maybe some fresh Maine lobster?

Maybe then she'd let her hair down again. Literally and figuratively.

"Vaughn."

There was a beautiful woman standing on my stoop. Glossy black hair and full lips, and I knew the swimsuit model body beneath her dress well. I stopped, my hand balling around my keys in my pocket. The pointy metal teeth bit into my palm.

"Alisha," I said, "What are you doing here?"

Just seeing her brought back a flood of memories.

"I heard you were in town and I needed to come and see you," she said, "I couldn't stop thinking about you. Don't tell me you never think about it."

"I don't," I said, starting up the steps. I intended on walking past and her getting into my house before she could get into my head.

But now I couldn't help it. It had been two years ago. Right before Stacey, now that I thought about it. Alisha had done some modeling promos for some piece of software I released and I'd met her at the after party for the shoot.

Things got hot and heavy fast. Then, like usual, they stopped dead.

I pulled my keys out and found the one for the door lock. Alisha put her hand on my wrist, stopping me. I looked down at her fingers. They were slender and pretty.

"This isn't a good idea, Alisha," I said.

"I just want to talk," she replied, her hand not

moving. This close, I could smell that perfume she knew I liked so much. I used to find it intoxicating. Now it just reminded me of something I'd rather forget.

"Talk about what?"

"Us," she said.

I recoiled. "There isn't any 'us,' and there hasn't been for a long time. Do us both a favor and stay away."

She got a stubborn cast in her eye. I recognized it. It had been one of the things that attracted me to her in the beginning. Now I knew it meant trouble. Trouble for me.

"You'll let me say my piece or I'll stand out here until you do."

I considered testing that challenge. I didn't want to deal with this sort of thing right now. But if I did leave her outside, I knew it would get out somehow. It always did. I checked my watch, reminding myself that there was still plenty of time before Quinn would be over.

However, I also knew that I'd hurt her when I slammed the brakes on that relationship. And she had left so quickly, like Stacey, that I never had the chance to try and explain myself, to offer an apology for being such a shoddy person.

I figured I owed her that much. My guilt demanded that much of me. I knew on the exterior I looked like the sort of person who didn't experience things like guilt. I did, though.

"You'll say your piece and then you'll go?" I said.

The hard, stubborn glint in her eyes softened and she smiled. "Yes, of course."

I slid the key into the lock and pushed the door open, then stepped back and waved her forward. "After you."

Even as I did it, it felt like a mistake. I put that down to how petty I could be. *Just tell her the truth and send her on her way.* I wanted to check my watch again, even though I just did it.

Hours. I have hours before Quinn gets here. Alisha will be gone by then.

Chapter 12

QUINN

Once again I found myself standing at the door to Vaughn Ward's brownstone. Like before, I gave it a disapproving look. How could a five star hotel not be good enough?

And the hotel had still charged C&M for Ward's entire stay, despite his checking out early. If he pulled his account, I was certain the blame for that extra bill would fall on my head, too.

And now I had other associations with this place. I could see the third floor window. There was a light on up there. I'd looked out of that window just moments before Ward had kissed me.

My lips tingled at the memory. It was a good kiss. And his hands had applied the right amount of pressure, holding me steady without hurting, showing the urgency of his desire.

It disturbed me how easily I recalled something I considered a mistake.

Will he try that again? I wondered. He might, even though I'd told him not to. *Come on, get this over with.* I thought. I tugged at my jacket, the USB stick in my pocket pushing against my palm.

Then I checked myself quickly in my reflection in the door. I kept my hair up. I had a nice, determined, no-BS look in my eyes. I needed to act before that expression cracked.

And hey, maybe I didn't look so bad. I examined my reflection further, trying to catch a glimpse of what Ward seemed to see.

I suppose if I pretended my nose was a little smaller and narrower, if my cheekbones were higher and more pronounced, I could be considered pretty. Maybe if I had my hair down, too…

My fingers twitched with the desire to reach up and pull these fresh pins out of my hair and let it tumble back to my shoulders. I stopped myself. *It doesn't matter. If I didn't have to do this for my job, I wouldn't be here right now.*

And that was also why I had forced Ward to leave before Trish might see him and get her claws into him. Yeah, that was why.

I reached for the doorbell but hesitated. *Why am I nervous?* It was true. Nervous wings fluttered around in my stomach, and I kept glancing at my reflection.

It's because I'm worried he might try something again, I told myself. But what if it was something else? What if it wasn't worry that he would try something, but rather excitement and anticipation of him trying again? *Preposterous*, I thought.

Is it? Is it really? I shook my head, trying to clear it. Then I forced myself to push the doorbell.

I thought he might answer right away. He was expecting me, after all. But he didn't. Then I remembered how he seemed to rejoice in frustrating my expectations of his behavior.

I hit the doorbell again, resolving to give him another 30 seconds before catching a taxi back to my condo.

"What is the holdup?" I muttered. I took a step back so that I could look up at that third floor window again. There was definitely a light on up there. Someone was home.

Though that wasn't necessarily true. Ward definitely had the money to leave a light on at home while he went out.

I turned and looked at the car parked by the curb in front of the brownstone's stoop. I wasn't really a car person. It looked expensive and sporty. And I think it had been parked there when I'd come here before. It was his.

I put it down to not wanting to take a taxi through the city at rush hour, but I went and tried his door.

82

It wasn't locked. It swung back and revealed that warm entrance hall I remembered.

Odd. I thought. This was a nice neighborhood and all, but people still locked their doors. Especially if they were out.

I went inside, closing the door behind me. "Ward? Are you here?"

Those wings in my stomach fluttered up a storm. This wasn't like me, going into someone's home uninvited. I didn't even like being in stores close to closing time. I always felt guilty, like the employees were trying to tell me to get the hell out with their polite smiles.

Still, it was such a nice house. I stood in the entryway, looking around at the retro wood paneling and those bits of modern abstract pieces Ward had chosen to set everything off.

I imagined what it might be like to live in a place like this. I knew if I made junior partner, senior partner wasn't that far behind. Mr. Callaghan was an old man. Mr. Montblanc was on vacation more often than not. I could get a place like this if I made the kind of money they made.

Unfortunately, Vaughn Ward stood watch at that particular gate. If this didn't go well, I could kiss all this goodbye.

Should I just leave the USB on a table somewhere with a note? That would serve me in two ways. It would show him that I'd been working on his account, for one. And that I'd fulfilled my part of the bargain and come back to his house despite my misgivings.

I started my search for paper when I heard something from upstairs. I took the stairs, sliding my hand along the rail. I walked quietly.

The higher I went, the clearer the sounds became. Voices. I recognized Ward's voice, but the other was unfamiliar and female.

My hackles started rising, that jealousy sparking in my chest. Totally irrational, I knew, but also totally unstoppable.

"You should leave," Vaughn said.

"Why?" the woman said, "Do you have another woman coming over?"

I knew that I should just continue on up. Tell Ward that his door was open and that I let myself in and hey, here's your USB stick. See ya. But I didn't. I paused on the stairs, holding my breath so that I could hear what they said better.

I shouldn't care that he had a woman up there with him. *Probably a hot one, too. An actress or a model or something.* It also shouldn't surprise me. From that whiff of perfume I got the night before, I knew he'd had a woman there before me.

If anything, this was good. It meant he was getting over me. Maybe he'd stop pressing me and let me do my work in peace.

It was what I wanted, wasn't it?

"The why of it is my business, not yours, Alisha," Vaughn replied.

"It is another woman. I can tell. Who is she?" Alisha said.

Alisha? I thought. I never liked that name. There'd been a girl named Alisha I went to high school with. A popular girl, pretty, all that. She'd called me Freckle-Face once in gym class at the beginning of senior year and the name had stuck.

Just thinking about it made my cheeks heat up in anger. I tried to not think about how my freckles showed up darker when I flushed like that.

Oh, so many years of insecurity from one little high school joke.

I didn't like this woman Vaughn had up there with him already.

"She's none of your concern, that's who she is," Vaughn said. I heard a leather creak and figured that he had just stood up from a couch or chair.

84

"I don't think any woman is a concern of yours, Vaughn. Not for long, anyway. I can see that this was a waste of time."

"I'm glad we both agree on something."

Another leather creak. Alisha standing up as well, probably. "You know what? I feel sorry for her, whoever she is. Sorry she'll have to discover just who you really are."

"I've explained myself to you about as much I feel like," Vaughn said, an edge in his voice, "I know things didn't end well between us, and I regret that. But I can't say I'll be sorry to see you leave. Here, I'll even show you where the door is in case you've forgotten."

Ouch, I thought. I kind of wished I could see the expression on Alisha's face.

"You're a wreck, Vaughn. Always have been, always will be," Alisha said.

"Tell me something I don't know. Now get out before I throw you out."

I felt the urge to defend Ward, to go up there and tell Alisha she should go mind her own business. Even though I knew I should be on her side, telling him where to shove it.

"Have a nice life, Vaughn," Alisha said. I heard her footsteps start towards the stairs.

The stairs, where I stood listening in on their private conversation.

I acted on impulse. "Ward, are you up there?" I said, pulling myself up the stairs. I reached the top, entering the third floor. Ward stood near the window. Alisha was closer. As I suspected, she was gorgeous.

She gave me a look that reminded me of the one I'd gotten from Stacey back at the hotel.

"Oh," I said, "I'm sorry, am I interrupting something? It's just that you wanted me to meet you here and I rang the bell a couple times. The door was open, and then I thought I heard voices…" I wondered if that sounded convincing. It was pretty close to the truth, anyway.

"You're not interrupting anything," Ward said, looking first at Alisha and then at me. It was a worried look.

Alisha shook her head at that. "Yeah, don't worry. That interruption happened a long time ago. You're tastes have changed, Vaughn." She let her eyes appraise me. I felt embarrassed in my own skin.

"I can give you this," I said, pulling the USB stick from my pocket and holding it up. "That way I can leave you two alone."

I looked at Alisha again and realized that I recognized her. She looked different with so much clothes on, but I remember admiring that glossy black mane of hers in various ad spreads.

That spark of jealousy burst into open flame. *How am I supposed to compete with* that? *I'm not competing, remember?* I wasn't certain that I'd convinced myself.

"Oh, don't worry, I was leaving," Alisha said. She winked at Vaughn and then walked to the stairs. When she started down them, she paused beside me and leaned closer. "Take it from me, sweetie, he's damaged goods."

She laughed a light, mirthless laugh as she continued down. I looked back at her, then to Ward. *Damaged goods? Who isn't?* I thought, knowing that I carried around my own fair share of baggage and hang-ups.

Not that I was looking for someone. Especially not someone like Vaughn Ward.

Ward wiped the worry from his expression and replaced it with his usual swagger. "This didn't go like I planned."

"So you're saying you don't normally have your ex-girlfriends over often?"

"She is my ex, yes. She won't be around anymore, though."

"Should I expect more to come out of the

woodwork? Because if you have so many personal matters to deal with, I'm sure it will cause delays. We can't go ahead with this material without your say so, remember," I said. I loved seeing him uncomfortable for once.

"Ah, no on the woodwork bit. At least, I hope not," he said. "You came, and I knew you would."

"Because you wouldn't leave my office," I said.

"Well, there's that, yeah. But I don't think that's the only reason you're back here."

From where I stood on the top stair, I could easily pick out the spot where we'd kissed. It was close. My skin tingled at the memory, pebbling with gooseflesh. "You're right. I came to show you some alterations I've made. I think they're good. But marketing is just like retail in that the customer is always right."

He looked at me. I could see him considering, thinking. I wondered what went on behind those wonderfully clear eyes of his.

Then, instead of replying, he turned around and went back over to the window. "I really do love this view. You know, if you hadn't had me put up in that hotel, I wouldn't have bought this place and this view. I really should thank you."

I grimaced. "No thanks necessary. Approval on these alterations, on the other hand…"

He didn't answer me. From here, I couldn't help noticing the figure he cut. Nice, broad shoulders and chest with tapered waist. I bet he had a six-pack underneath that shirt, too.

And a great butt, too. I bet it was nice and firm…

I shook my head. *God, I'm behaving like Anne!* It was almost magical, this man's effects on women.

Fine, if he wants me to come up there with him I'll go up there. But only to give him the USB stick! Besides, from that close I could keep my eyes from admiring his body. I hoped I could, anyway.

So I sighed, took another breath, and went up there. I

stopped beside him. He didn't look at me. I could see our translucent reflections in the window glass.

I could smell him, too. Ward seemed to be of the less is more school when it came to cologne. Enough scent to give a hint, to make you want more. *Probably another way he gets women to come closer to him.*

"Here," I said, "Take it." I offered the USB stick, the little metal connector on the end catching some of the light from the sunset.

Vaughn reached, his fingers wrapping around mine. His skin was soft and warm against mine. That warmth made me swallow. I didn't pull back.

We looked out the window a little while longer before his eyes turned to me. They weren't as clear as I'd first thought. No, there was a storm in them. A storm that threatened to consume him and then me. My mouth went dry. My lips parted slightly.

He still didn't let go of my hand. "Quinn," he said.
"Yes?"

"I want you. And I know you want me, too."

"Do you?" I replied. That heat from his hand started spreading through me. I tried telling myself that I did want him, but only on a physical level. Who wouldn't? But part of being an adult was knowing when to ignore what you wanted.

I could tell myself whatever I wanted and it didn't have any effect. This close, he was magnetic. Little electric tingles kept running across the surface of my skin, awakening all my senses.

It was like my body wanted to feel every sensation it could, and to the fullest extent. The past and the future closed off, leaving only the present. The world shrank until only Ward and I occupied it.

I wanted to pull my hand out of his, but I didn't. I didn't want him to kiss me again, but I did.

I wanted that and more. I wanted all of it; I wanted all of him. I took a deep breath, but it didn't steady me at all.

"I do. You know, since we met I don't think more than a few minutes have gone by without you in my thoughts," he said.

We still didn't look at each other. We both seemed to know that if we let our eyes meet we wouldn't be able to stop what happened after.

I could look at his reflection safely, though, and I did. "It's only been a few days," I said, "You hardly know me. How can you think you want me so much?"

"Some things you just know right away," he replied. His reflected face grinned.

"We shouldn't," I said, wondering if I was trying to convince him or myself. *Maybe both.*

"Will you try and stop me?" Ward asked, his eyes regarding my reflection. I didn't reply, because I didn't know the answer.

Then he stopped looking at my reflection and looked at the real me instead. I wished he wouldn't; my reflection looked so much nicer than the real me. It was so vague you couldn't see the freckles, for one. And it softened all the lines I thought were too harsh.

"Quinn," Ward said, urging me to look at him, to let myself fall under the spell of his charm again.

Don't, I thought. But my willpower melted fast. I turned towards him. I don't know if his hand actually became hotter against mine or if I just thought it did. Either way, his fingers burned.

I kept my eyes on the collar of his shirt. He kept the top three buttons undone, giving me a glimpse of what looked like sculpted muscle. It was tantalizing, I admit. And much easier to look at than his eyes.

He cupped my cheek like he did before, tilting my head back.

When our eyes met, a cold tremble ran through me. It was fear and anticipation and desire all in one. My lips parted and I breathed sharply through them.

"Ward…" I said, my eyes searching his. That storm I

89

saw earlier had built to even greater proportion in him. I could feel its intensity washing over me, ready to drown me in its deluge.

"Call me Vaughn," he said, "Or I'll start calling you Miss Windsor."

I thought he might kiss me right away, but he didn't. I didn't know if it was a calculated move or not, but it made every nerve in my body sing. He kept looking at me, letting his eyes scan my face.

It was like he was trying to commit every contour to memory. I couldn't remember the last time any man had looked at me, really looked at me, like that.

"I don't want to be just another one of your conquests," I said.

"And what if I wanted you to be my final one?" he replied.

I didn't have anything to say to that. I thought he might kiss me then, but he still refrained. Instead, he finally released my hand from his. My skin prickled at the sudden sensation of cold.

"What..." I asked when he started lifting that hand.

But then I knew what he wanted to do. He reached up and plucked the pins from my hair again. Once more, my hair tumbled down to my shoulders.

My breathing became faster. I couldn't get enough air. The room felt ten degrees hotter than before.

He cupped my other cheek so that my face tilted back slightly in his hands. Without really thinking about it, I slipped my hands around his waist, between his jacket and his shirt.

I could feel the warmth of his body, feel the way his torso expanded and then shrank with each breath.

He smiled. It wasn't one of his crooked, roguish ones this time. It was a real smile. "You haven't told me to stop."

"You're right, I haven't," I replied.

And then he did press his mouth to mine. We fit

together so nicely. My eyes closed, letting me better concentrate on the sensation of his lips against mine.

Again, they were gentle yet insistent. Hot with desire. His stubble prickled me lightly. My fingers squeezed into his sides when the full force of the kiss hit me.

Electricity crackled within us, that storm building in intensity, crossing from him to me over and over.

A ball of heat burned inside me, down low and getting lower with each beat of my heart.

Then his hands left my face. He traced his fingers down my shoulders, down my arms. Reaching my waist, he pushed his hands between my blouse and my jacket. Then he pulled me hard against him.

His mouth slid off mine, moving down my jaw to my throat. His hot breaths washed over my skin again and again.

"You are so hot," he said. Then he pulled my blouse up out of my pants. His fingertips ran along the bare strip of skin he'd revealed along my hips. His touch made my skin tingle.

I loved feeling his hands explore me. I loved how his touch made me buzz with desire inside.

His hands slid down from my hips, cupping my ass. He continued kissing my neck, nuzzling his mouth against me. He squeezed and I gasped.

"Tell me you want me," he said between kisses. One hand stayed on my ass while the other slid down my thigh. He grabbed my knee and pulled it up along his body, forcing us closer together.

"Tell me," he said again, his voice insistent, laden with the need to hear me say the words.

He let my leg drop slowly, then he ran both hands up my back, under my blouse. The warmth from his palms soaked into me, almost matching the heat that burned inside of me.

I wanted to tell him I that I did want him. I wanted to so badly. But I couldn't stop my mind from calling up

Stacey telling me to be careful, or Alisha, telling me to stay away.

And I could still smell Alisha's perfume in the room. What kind of man was Ward? The kind of man who seduced women and then left them. The kind of man I shouldn't be around. The kind of man I told myself I'd never be with again.

But his hands feel so nice. And his kisses along the delicate skin of my throat were the perfect mix of insistent and gentle. The softness of his lips and the prickle of his stubble intoxicated me, and I wanted to feel him slide those lips all over my body.

I knew he wanted to feel that, too.

He started unbuttoning my blouse, started letting his lips slide down between my breasts, which heaved with every deep breath I took to try and supply my body with all the air it craved.

"Say it," Ward said.

It took everything I had to push him away. Without our bodies pressing together, I felt cold. My desire cried out within me to grab him and hold him close again, but I resisted.

"No," I said. That ball of heat inside me dissolved, sending tendrils of warmth up into my skin. My lips felt raw and tender. "I don't want this."

"Yes, you do," Ward said. He took a step towards me and I took a step back. When he saw that, he stopped.

I did and I didn't. I needed time to collect myself, so I turned away from him. I redid the buttons he'd undone on my blouse. From the corners of my eyes I could see my hair hanging loose around my shoulder.

I still had the hair elastic in my pocket from the previous night, so I took it out and put my hair back in a ponytail. It would do, for now.

"Quinn, stop lying to yourself," Ward said.

I couldn't look at him. Not yet. So I stared out at the wall. It was a raw brick one, and my eyes wandered over the little gaps in the mortar. "Am I the one lying to myself? Are you sure you aren't? I think you're searching for something, but not even you are sure what it is. And every time you don't find it, you push the other person away without considering their feelings. And I can't be hurt like that."

Not again, I added, but in my mind only. *Everyone has baggage*, I thought, remembering the way Alisha told me Ward was damaged.

"But it would be so good. We both know that," Ward said. I could feel him standing behind me, his presence solid and large. My body ached, and I wanted him to wrap his arms around me and pull me against him again. I knew I couldn't let him, though.

"Just because something would be good doesn't mean that it's also right," I said. I hoped he understand the difference.

Tension built behind me. I could feel it so that the hairs on the back of my neck stood. And then it dissipated.

Ward didn't say anything. He turned around and went and sat on the couch, throwing his arms across the back.

My knees trembled for a few seconds while my body calmed down. Now that all that warmth was gone, everything felt cold. I even did up a couple buttons on my jacket.

And it was still light outside. I thought it was funny how something important could feel like it lasted forever but in actuality probably only took a few minutes.

Be professional, I thought. It was a ridiculous thought, I knew, but I needed something to fall back on. Something to keep me from thinking about what might have happened.

I looked at Ward, and Ward looked at me. At first, I thought he might apologize. He didn't. I suppose he was one of those types who didn't see the need to apologize for the way they felt, for following their desires.

"If we go down to your study, I can show you my

proposed changes," I said, wanting nothing less than to leave this house. I knew I couldn't though. Not if I wanted to keep my job.

"I don't really care about that right now," Ward said. He looked back over his shoulder out the window. We both got quiet so that the dull noises from the street reached us. The hum of an engine. Someone laughing as they walked by.

"Then I'll go, and later I can send you a message with the details," I said, not liking that feeling of emptiness stretching between us.

Of course, home didn't sound that great, either. I would be alone there. Unless Mary asked me to watch the kids again. I really did need to go and adopt a cat or something.

"No," Ward said, "I have a better idea."

"What might that be?"

"There's a pub down at that corner I've been meaning to try. A few drinks sound really nice to me right now. And I think you'd be lying if you disagreed on that point."

I felt wary, but at the same time I admitted he was right. If there was ever a time I needed a drink or two it was right then. It might give me a sense of warmth inside, however false, to replace the coldness.

"Fine. Just drinks, though. Nothing else."

"Just drinks," he said, nodding.

We went down the stairs. I kept thinking how strange it was that someone like Vaughn Ward wanted to go someone as pedestrian as a corner pub. Judging by what I'd seen of him so far – driving expensive cars, buying expensive houses on a whim, dating beautiful and famous women – he'd want to go to some fancy restaurant.

But I guess I was wrong about him in that way. Which made me wonder what else I might be wrong about.

Chapter 13

VAUGHN

We got to the pub and seated ourselves on stools at the bar. It was a nice place, as far as pubs went. Very Irish feeling with its Irish flag hanging behind the bar, and little leprechaun ornaments at various places. There was a digital countdown to St. Patrick's Day as well.

The place smelled like Guinness and felt a touch too commercial, but I didn't mind. There were only a few other people in the booths, and no one else at the bar.

"What now?" Quinn said.

The stool was high enough that her feet dangled off the floor. When she swung her head to look around, her ponytail swished back and forth. I wanted to reach out and catch it.

Instead I curled my fists against my thighs. I kept thinking about how nice she smelled, and the way her skin had pebbled into gooseflesh when I touched it with my lips.

I kept thinking about the way she sucked her breath in through her teeth when I ran my hands up her back.

And I kept thinking about how she was probably right. I had a lot of wreckage in my wake, and I didn't want to make her a part of that.

"Drinks," I said. "What else?"

The bartender was a pretty redhead who came over when I made eye contact with her. Almost without thinking, I slipped into my normal way of interacting with good-looking women. A crooked smile and a casual attitude.

"What do you need?" she said, leaning against the bar. She wore a blouse like the one Quinn had on. Except she had it unbuttoned a fair way down, and when she leaned forward she wasn't shy about displaying her assets.

"I don't know, what do you have that you think I'd like?" I said, letting my smile widen just a touch. I kept my eyes on her face, which I knew she found interesting.

And then I noticed Quinn giving me a slight shake of the head, as though she expected nothing less.

I snapped out of it, leaning back from the bar. I ordered us a pitcher of beer, asking for whatever was most popular on tap and hoping it wasn't Coors Light.

The bartender looked disappointed.

"This reminds me of college," I said, looking around the pub some more. Lots of wood paneling. I guess everyone who lived in Back Bay loved wood paneling. At least it made the place feel warm.

"I can see it now," Quinn said. "Sorority sisters and waitresses fighting for your attention. A party everywhere you go."

The bartender put a sloshing pitcher of beer down in front of us and pulled two frosted mugs up from beneath the counter, finishing it off with a little glass bowl in the shape of a four-leaf clover filled to the prim with unshelled peanuts.

Quinn's comment earned a rueful laugh from me. This felt good, just sitting here with it. Normal, somehow. Familiar. Even though I'd never been to this place before and had known Quinn for about a week.

"Pretty opposite of that, actually. I'm one of those late-bloomer types, if you can believe it." I poured us each a beer, tilting the glasses to avoid too much foam.

"That I don't believe," she said. She kept looking at herself in the mirror behind the liquor bottles. It wasn't out of vanity, I could tell that.

It was a self-deprecating look I knew well. That manner of picking out every little perceived flaw and imperfection. She was hard on herself, I could tell.

And that discipline was what got her to where she was. Her bosses spoke highly of her, and even if I hadn't wanted her I would have let her handle my account.

"It's that same discipline that lifted you up that's holding you back," I said.

Quinn started, glancing at me and then at the mirror. She blushed when she realized that I'd caught her. "I'm not a narcissist, I swear."

"I know. But sometimes a little narcissism goes a long way. You have to appreciate yourself before other people will."

"Thanks for the pep talk," she said, bringing the mug to her lips. She was careful to wipe away the foam mustache left behind, I noticed.

I admired her profile while she let me, her nose and her cheekbones and her lips. I considered telling her again that she was beautiful, but I still didn't think she would believe it.

"You need to give yourself a little freedom. Some slack. That's where you'll find that things really start to come together," I said.

"Is that how you did it?" she said, glancing at me and then away again.

I looked around the pub and took a mouthful of beer. It bubbled against my tongue and tasted of hops, leaving a sharp aftertaste when I swallowed. Yes, this place did remind me of college.

Except I wished it didn't. "Something like that. Too much slack, maybe."

It was my turn to look in the mirror behind the bottles. I had to peer around an enormous Crown Royal, and then between two tall, frosted Smirnoffs.

I recognized the face staring back at me, but didn't. What was it? The 17th most beautiful? The face of a man who'd built his own company from the ground up, who could buy this entire block of buildings without any appreciable dent in his cash flow.

He was a man I didn't know. A man I never really expected to become.

I could still see the college kid in there somewhere. The one with an idea for an app he thought might make him a few bucks. Maybe enough for some beer every few weeks.

I didn't want to think about that anymore. I looked back to Quinn, who set down her mug half empty. I refilled it for her and topped mine up as well.

I caught that fiery bartender stealing glances at me from the corner where she wiped at the already clean countertop. I knew I could just give in and have her in my bed tonight, maybe forget about things for a while. I didn't want to do that anymore, either.

"So who hurt you?" I said.

She jerked like I'd smacked her, some amber beer sloshing over into a frothy puddle on the bar. "Who said anyone hurt me?" She glanced around the bar like I'd just given some secret away to the world.

Normally I liked surprising her. This time I didn't. "I'm guessing someone I remind you of in some way," I continued.

"You don't know what you're talking about," Quinn said.

"Takes a wreck to know a wreck," I replied, "Maybe if you just let somebody in it will help…"

I trailed off when she turned on me with fire in her eyes and a cruel smile on her lips. "Really?" she said. "And does it help you, letting all those women in? Do you even know how many anymore? Do you even care? Or are all you after is a quick fix? I'm sorry, I don't want to throw people away like they're empty, used syringes."

I got angry. Heat flared up in my chest and I squeezed the handle of my mug beer sloshed down the sides. A dozen different rebuttals ended on the tip of my tongue, ready to lash out like whips.

"So who hurt *you*?" Quinn asked, "Who are you trying to forget and get away from? Easy to ask, not so easy to answer, you see?"

My anger turned to sooty cinders at the back of my throat. I tried quenching the last few embers with another mouthful of draft. The sharpness of the aftertaste helped.

"You know, I could say that you're trying to avoid the question by throwing it back in my face."

Her jaw clenched, and that fire glowed behind her eyes. But the glow died down and she turned away from me again. I couldn't help thinking how beautiful she looked when she was angry. And the sadness hanging from her expression now didn't diminish it.

"Why are you doing this?" she asked. "I'm not worth it."

"I don't think you know what you're worth," I replied. My body ached for her. I wanted her so badly. I wanted to take her back to the brownstone and tear all her clothes off and not stop with her until we were both lying on my bed, panting and sweaty from the exertion. Make her forget whatever her worry was. Push away the memories.

It was a deep ache. And one I knew probably wouldn't be relieved. *But am I trying to help her forget, or am I just trying to help myself?*

The beer started buzzing in my brain, leaving a warm, thick halo around my head.

"Because I think it's what we both need," I said. I caught her eyes with mine and didn't let go.

Hers were an earthy green, reminding me of the color of mid-summer leaves right after a rain shower. A green that was deeper than it first appeared. There was no sign of that fire anymore, and I knew she'd pushed it back down to smolder inside of her.

She tore away from me. "This was a bad idea."

"Coming to the bar?" I said.

"Agreeing to this job. Thanks for the drink, I guess. I'm going home."

She got up. I thought about reaching out to her, asking her not to go yet. *Why does it matter so much?* I wondered. *Just let her go.*

Part of it was that I knew she expected me to do that. And I also knew that if I did she might stay. But I'd made a habit of defying expectations, and bad habits were always the hardest to break.

So I didn't reach out.

"If you get lonely I'm sure you won't have any problems finding some company," Quinn said, glancing pointedly in the direction of the bartender.

She moved to storm out of the bar. However, she only reached the booth nearest the door when she stopped. I thought I heard her mutter something, but couldn't quite make it out.

I thought it might be something like, *Be professional,* but I couldn't be certain.

She pulled something out of her pocket and came back towards me.

Unable to help myself, my heart started pounding. I thought that maybe she might have reconsidered.

"I almost forgot this," she said. She put her closed fist down on the bar, forced her fingers open, and pulled her hand back. The jump drive was there. "Please email me your thoughts on my suggestions. We're getting closer to the deadline."

I wanted to say something, but couldn't. My mind couldn't find the words to express what I felt. She watched me, waiting.

This was it, I knew. I could open up to her. Tell her things I hadn't told anyone, not even Stacey or Alisha. Things I thought she could understand. I couldn't, though. Just the thought of it gave me palpitations.

Finally, unable to do more than groan inwardly, I responded with a crooked smile.

She shook her head and then looked over at the bartender, "He's all yours. Have fun."

I watched Quinn leave the bar, that ponytail of hers swishing from the force of her footsteps. From the corner of my eye, I saw the bartender lean back over the counter, clasping her hands close to where my sweating mug of beer sat.

"I'm Ricki," she said, "Has anyone told you lately how handsome you are?"

God damn it, Quinn, I thought, *Why did you do that?* And then, *Why did I do that?*

Chapter 14

QUINN

I couldn't get that stupid bartender out of my head. She'd seen me get up to go and swooped in on Ward like a vulture on some tasty piece of meat.

Well, more specifically, I couldn't get the image of that bartender's cleavage out of my mind, and the way it popped when she leaned over the bar like that.

I'd wanted to tell her to take a hike, but couldn't. Not after Ward had the nerve to smile at me like that. Like he didn't even care.

I marched up the street, looking for a taxi. Of course the taxis never came to this neighborhood much. Everyone here owned an Audi or three. Who needed a taxi?

You just go have fun with that redhead, then, I thought with a mental sneer. I started wondering how bad things would be if I went to Ms. Spencer tomorrow and told her I wanted off the Phoenix Software account.

Probably pretty bad. But beer from the bar swam in my head, and I let the fantasy entertain me for a while.

Normally I didn't do much drinking. I ended up taking my work home so often that I needed my head as clear as possible. Well, that, and I usually looked after the kids for Mary at least once a week.

I turned back once and looked toward the corner pub. What had he meant with all that talk about discipline? He'd gotten nostalgic in there, turning into someone I could relate to.

It was just another one of his tactics to try and get me in the sack, I figured. We'd come so close back on the third floor of the brownstone and he hadn't want to give in so quickly.

I couldn't help wondering what it might like to be with him. Especially not with the warm fuzz from the beer filling my head. He knew how to kiss. He knew how to use his mouth. The way he touched me brought my body alive with desire.

And we hadn't even taken off any clothes. I couldn't help fantasizing about being held in his strong arms, both our bodies slick with sweat as we slid together.

The thing was, I knew I wanted that to happen. Some parts of me more than others. And at this point all my reasons not to no longer rang true, but hollow instead. Yet, in spite of that, I'd turned him down again.

Better be careful. Soon enough I bet he'll stop trying.

Wasn't that what I wanted, though? Him to stop trying, to leave me alone and in peace?

I thought so. I used to think so.

What I really wanted to know was how he managed to hit so close to the mark with his questions. *But how could he possibly know anything about my past?*

Maybe the two of us were opposite sides of one coin. He responded to his own inner turmoil, burying it with a never-ending parade of beautiful women. I responded to mine by shutting men out before they could get too close.

I wondered if that was what I sensed in him, a sort of sympathy, that I reacted to so harshly, that made me dislike him so strongly?

He's probably still in the bar, I thought, *I could go back in and find out.* But part of me feared that I might got back in there and find him with his arms around that pretty redhead's waist, his lips locked to hers. And I don't think I could have stood that.

I walked three blocks before I saw a yellow cab. It was already engaged, so I needed to wait for a second, which I caught.

***

Three days later I went down to the art department to talk with Anne about a couple layouts.

A couple of her fellow artists sat at their tables, their tongues clenched gently between their teeth while they plied their trade.

Anne herself sat in front of that bank of monitors, experimenting with different filters on the image of a smiling boy. She wore her headphones as usual, a tinny bass beat emitting from them.

I touched her shoulder and she turned, frowning, at the interruption. When she saw me the frown flipped to a smile and she slipped her headphones down so they rested around her neck.

"How are things going with you and Mr. Hotstuff?"

I shrugged. "They're not going anywhere. I don't think I've talked to him in three days or so. Unless you count emails back and forth."

"That depends. Are they steamy emails, like with naughty pictures and that sort of thing?"

"Definitely not!" I said, heat rushing to my face. "They're just about the account. Progress reports, samples, that sort of thing."

Anne pouted, disappointed, "That's such a shame."

I'd come down intending on speaking with her about the color choices in an ad scheduled to run in next month's issue of *Wired*, but now I had to know what she was going on about.

"What do you mean?" I said. I kept thinking, *Be professional*, but it didn't have its usual effect on me. I glanced back at the other members of the art department, but their work preoccupied them.

I wished I could lose myself in something like that so easily.

"I mean that you guys have something!"

That heat started in my cheeks again. "Yes, we have a business relationship. He's my client. That's it."

"That's not what I saw when he came by."

I snorted, "I'm surprised you saw anything but Ward. You were like one of those cartoon characters whose eyes turn into throbbing hearts and your tongue unrolls down to your feet."

It was Anne's turn to blush. She was pretty. "Can you blame me?"

With no effort at all, I remembered the heat of Ward's mouth against mine, the pulse of hot desire through my body, how close I came to giving in to him. "No," I admitted, "I suppose that I can't."

She stuck her tongue out at me and we both laughed before continuing. "No, I definitely sensed something. He definitely has a thing for you. Guys don't just drop in like that to check up on business stuff."

"They do if they're mega-wealthy CEOs with a lot riding on their next product release," I said. The excuse sounded hollow even to me.

"Please," Anne said, screwing up her face. "I'm right and you're wrong. And you know what else? I think you have a thing for him, too."

I snorted. "In his dreams, maybe. I can't help the way he might feel, but I'm a *professional*. I don't get into that sort of thing. It would violate our business relationship."

Anne gave me a look that asked me if I really believed the words coming out of my mouth. I had to admit that I wasn't certain I could use the business relationship argument anymore. Not when we'd kissed twice and I could recall the exact pressure of his hand on my ass.

"You're different since you got that account," Anne said.

"What? No way. Okay, maybe I haven't been sleeping as much, but can you blame me! My whole career's on the line here…"

"No, no. That's not what I'm talking about. And I don't mean it in a bad way. Not at all. You've changed."

"Name one way," I said, crossing my arms tight enough that my shoulder blades hurt.

"You're wearing your hair down, for one," Anne said, nodding at me.

I reached up and touched the locks of hair lying against my shoulder. I glanced away from her. "Yeah, well, it's just getting a little long for the bun and like I said I'm kind of pressed for time to go to the salon."

"Yes, it couldn't possibly be because you know he likes it when you have it down. Not at all. Anyway, it's not just that. You're happier, too."

I raised my eyebrow at that. "Ridiculous. I don't think I've met a more infuriating man in my life. Besides, if this goes well it means I'll make *junior partner*, Anne. The thought of a promotion makes me happy. Not him."

She gave me her *Please* look again. *You know, she has a point*, I started thinking. I stopped that train of thought in its tracks. I'd given her perfectly reasonable explanations and she could take them or leave them.

"Shall I continue?" Anne said, an evil grin accompanying the question.

"No," I said, "Can we talk about something at work actually related to our jobs now?"

"Sure, right after Trish leaves."

"Nice to see you, too, hipster. I have a bone to pick with you about some concept pieces," Trish said.

My stomach sank. I turned around to face her.

"Quinn? I almost didn't recognize you from the back. You actually look a little bit like a girl today. How are things going with Vaughn Ward? Ready to move over and put him into the hands of someone who knows how to take care of his needs?"

I knew she was trying to get a rise out of me. I knew inside she was jealous of me and resented that I was better at this job than she was.

No rational thought could keep me from boiling over, though. "Phoenix Software is already being taken care of the way it deserves," I said, surprised at my own ability to refrain from telling her that she *actually looked a little bit* like she'd just walked in off whatever corner she normally worked.

But hey, go me. Go willpower.

The corner of Trish's mouth twitched and she looked me up and down. "You know, you're definitely not his type anyway. I don't see why you're even bothering with the hair. Ever heard of a straightener, by the way? Because every other woman in Boston has. But hey, keep going like that and I'm sure Ward will be requesting a replacement any time now. So disregard my straightener advice, please."

I wanted to reach up and touch my hair in indignation. My gorge started rising, the hurt and anger threatening to burn right through my cheeks.

Trish basked in the warmth of that and I knew I'd let her win again. I swallowed against the lump in my throat and turned back to Anne. "I'll come back later."

Anne winked at me and said so that only I could hear, "Don't worry, I'll put her work at the bottom of the pile."

"Can you hurry it up?" Trish said, "Some of us actually have work to do."

"Yes," I replied, "Some of us do."

I left the art department with all my blood boiling. *She'll get Vaughn over my dead body.*

That thought stopped me in my tracks right in the middle of the hall. The intern pushing the mail cart behind me had to jerk to a halt to avoid running me over.

"Sorry," I said, stepping out of the way and leaning against the wall. I didn't think I could still feel so jealous and protective of Ward, not after our little chat at the bar.

More than that, I'd called him Vaughn. I never called him Vaughn, not even to his face. Always *Ward* or *Mr. Ward.*

Vaughn Ward, who hadn't tried to contact me except to reply to my emails telling me he approved of my changes and suggestions to the upcoming ad campaign.

I did touch my hair, then. *Maybe Anne's right.* Ward seemed to be keeping his distance now. Just like I'd always told him I wanted.

But if that was what I wanted, then why did I let my hair down? Why did I nearly explode in an angry fireball at the mere suggestion that I might lose him to Trish?

Not lose him. Lose the account. I corrected myself. It didn't feel so correct, though.

Finally, after three days, I let myself express the thought that had been lurking in the back of my mind since I'd stormed out of the bar.

Why hasn't he tried to see me again? I also remembered thinking that if I kept pushing him away he'd stay away for good. Was I already passed that point?

I told him I wasn't worth it. Does he believe it now? My heart sank at that suggestion.

I don't know why I did it, but I went back to my desk and started researching him. Not his company, not his success, but him.

I typed his name into the Google Image Search and started scrolling through the results, my chin resting against my knuckles.

Work, you should be doing work, I thought, making some token attempt to pull myself away from the search. *This is a kind of work. Understanding your client helps you meet their needs better.*

It was a weak excuse. How could an image of Ward at a red carpet event, or this one here of him in the stands at a baseball game, help me with ad material for Phoenix Software?

Still, I had to admit that I liked looking through the pictures. He was a good looking man. I wasn't even certain what I was hoping to find, or what I was looking for. Just something.

And not seeing him in three days did get to me, a little. Maybe I wasn't as googly-eyed about it Anne, but I still found him attractive.

On a whim, I set the date filter back several years.

There weren't very many pictures. This would have

been from around the time he was finishing college and I was just starting, I realized.

"What is this?" I said, perking up. One picture in particular caught my attention. I clicked on it, making it bigger.

It was a somewhat typical college picture. Three guys, clearly friends, their arms across each other's shoulders. The young man in the middle bore a striking resemblance to a certain cocky, full-of-himself CEO I knew.

"It can't be..." I muttered, squinting and leaning forward.

I remembered characterizing who I thought Ward had been in college to him at that pub. Handsome, cocky, a stick in one hand to beat away all the co-eds throwing themselves at him.

Then again, Ward had also scoffed at that notion. And now I saw why.

The man I saw in the picture was good looking. Or he would be, if he'd known how to dress, how to do his hair, that sort of thing. In the picture was a young man who was handsome and didn't know it.

His smile was full and too innocent. His hair was too long, the scruff on his cheeks and chin too scruffy. And it looked like sometime between then and now he'd decided to pack some muscle on. His shirt was too baggy and clashed with his skin tone.

If I'd seen him at school I would have thought he was a member of the A/V or computer club.

I probably would have found him cute, too. The kind of cute guy who, when he got invited to parties, spent the whole time glued to the wall, trying to screw up the courage to talk to that girl he had a crush on from his English 101 lectures.

Not for the first time, I thought that I didn't know who Vaughn Ward was. Maybe no one did. The picture in question was hosted on what looked like a long-forgotten college forum, so it wasn't like people saw it every day or something.

What happened to him? I wondered. Whoever he was then, he seemed happier than who he'd become now.

I leaned back in my chair, trying to process the image. I had to smile, too; he still surprised me at every turn.

"Who are you, Vaughn Ward?" I said.

My phone rang, the sudden noise making me jerk in my chair. I answered it, my heart thumping against my ribs. My eyes kept straying to the screen.

"Quinn, please come up to my office as soon as you can." It was Ms. Spencer. Something in her tone made a pit open in my stomach.

"Of course, I'll be right up. Can I ask what this is about?" I said.

"It's better we talk in person. I'll expect you shortly," she replied. Then she hung up.

I pulled the phone from my ear and frowned at it. *What's going on?* Ms. Spencer usually only met with me to discuss the results of my projects. She tried not to micromanage her employees, preferring to give them leeway.

People needed freedom to be their most creative, she told me.

I started closing the internet browser on my computer, getting ready to go. Then I clicked the picture and saved it to my hard drive. It was an old forum it was hosted on, who knew when someone might decide to take everything down?

When I got up to Ms. Spencer's office I found her sitting behind her desk, as usual. She looked up at me over the rims of her glasses and I couldn't decipher her expression.

For a panicked moment, I thought that maybe Trish's threat had been prophetic. That maybe Ward had decided that he didn't want me on his account anymore and that Ms. Spencer wanted to break the news to me in person.

Please don't let that be it, I thought. Then I knew it

wasn't the thought of losing the account and the potential promotion that made the pit in my stomach widen, it was the idea of not getting to see Ward again.

"You've changed your hair," she said.

Unconsciously, I reached up with one hand and touched my hair, "Yes. I… haven't had time to go to the salon," I replied, giving her the same excuse that I'd given Anne.

I suppose if I said it enough times I might actually start to believe it myself. "Is there something wrong?" I asked, wanting to get to the point. I couldn't help feeling nervous. I liked Ms. Spencer, thought of her as my mentor, even, but she intimidated me.

"I'm not sure," she replied, sitting back in her chair and pushing her glasses back up her nose, "Is there one?"

I shook my head. "No, everything's going great, actually. We're on target for all the ads. Mr. Ward has approved the press release we'll be sending out shortly. If anything, I think we're actually ahead of schedule."

Ms. Spencer smiled. The expression took ten years off her face, and I saw how pretty she was. With her hands on her desk like they were, I also saw no rings on any of her fingers. *Makes sense, I mean she is* Ms. *Spencer, not* Mrs.

I don't know why that little detail chose that moment to surface in my thoughts. Then again, many unexpected things had happened to me over the past couple of weeks.

"I've kept my eye on you since you started here. You probably realize that," Ms. Spencer said. "And I have to say, you remind me a lot of myself."

I couldn't tell if she meant that as a compliment or not, and therefore couldn't decide whether I should thank her for the comparison. I stayed quiet, instead.

Ms. Spencer regarded me for a little before continuing. "And since it's so unprecedented to have such a junior employee handle such an important account, I agreed with Mr. Callaghan and the other partners when they said we should keep a closer eye on you than usual."

Something about that made my mouth and throat go dry. "What does that mean?" I kept thinking that I must have screwed up somewhere. Forgotten some important step. Spent too much money buying airtime or ad space. Something.

Ms. Spencer kept looking at me, and I could tell she was trying to decide on what to do. I felt so in the dark.

Finally, she stood up. She was a bit shorter than me, a bit slighter.

"You're familiar with the term 'opportunity cost,' correct? The idea that by choosing one course of action you do so at the cost of other courses you might have taken?"

"Yes," I said, trying not to frown. It was a concept that had come up a fair amount while I was getting my undergraduate degree. By choosing one thing, you take away your ability to choose certain other things. Pretty simple, pretty obvious.

But why is she bringing this up now? Am I in trouble or aren't I in trouble?

"I don't normally get this personal with coworkers, so please forgive me," Ms. Spencer said. She walked over to a bookcase against one wall of her office and looked at the spines of the books sitting on it without really seeing them.

I still didn't know what to say, how to react, or even what was going on, so I stayed silent.

"As I said, you remind me a lot of myself at your age. Though I also have to say, and not without some jealousy, that I think you're ahead of where I was," she said as she ran her fingers along the spines of the books. "I wanted to be the top person in my field. And I wasn't going to let anything get in my way. Nothing at all, you understand? A one-track mind."

"I understand," I said. Some of the things she said sounded like compliments, but I got the impression that she didn't mean them as compliments. Not in this context, at least.

113

"Taking that particular path cost me many opportunities that, now that I'm not so far from retirement as I would like, I wish I'd reconsidered. Because I have to say, I've had more success than many other people. But I find myself asking one question more and more often. At what cost? Can you tell me, Quinn?"

She looked back over her shoulder at me, so I didn't think it was a rhetorical question. "You have to make sacrifices, I suppose."

"You name it and I sacrificed it," she said. "I couldn't come home for either of my parents' funerals. Important business meetings with important clients, you see. I haven't even received cards for Christmas or anything like that from my sister in a good ten years. There was a young man I used to know. He told me he loved me and I loved him, too. I really did. But I let him slip through my fingers, too. Opportunity cost, you see."

"I'm sorry," I said, not knowing what else to say to her.

"You and me both," she replied, "A career like this costs so much. Too much, for some. I'm proud of what I've accomplished, but so often lately I find myself regretting what those accomplishments took away from me."

She moved away from the bookshelf and stood in front of me. I could pick out the grey strands in her hair from this close, see the fine wrinkles at the corners of her eyes. "Some might look and say that I've made no mistakes, simply choices that took me down on life path rather than another."

"What do you say?" I asked. The question sounded a little too impertinent to me, but I asked it anyway.

Ms. Spencer nodded, "Sometimes I think one way, sometimes I think the other. But by now I figure you're probably wondering what all my rambling has to do with you."

It would definitely have been impertinent to answer

that question, so I choose discretion. She looked at me, and I felt something like a fresh recruit being dressed down by the grizzled sergeant.

"Well, here it is," she said. "I wished I'd had someone to lay this out to me when I was as young as you are. So I decided I'd lay it out for you. Since you started on the Ward account, I've noticed how much time you spend outside of regular office hours on work. Email access logs and the like, you see. Don't worry, I just see the access and usage reports, not your actual emails or anything like that."

I struggled to find some sort of excuse. "I want to make sure the job's done right. Like you told me before, doing well could really give me career a boost."

She gave me a sharp look and I quieted.

"I've also made certain other inquiries. I got curious when Mr. Callaghan described how... vehement Vaughn Ward was that you handle the account."

"I'm not being removed from the account?" I said, my nerves jagged inside of me.

"What? No, of course not. I wanted to share my own experiences with you and make sure you understood the opportunity cost of being totally professional, totally career-oriented."

She raised her eyebrow, and I got the sense that she'd inferred quite a bit of the tension between Ward and me, much like Anne. However, unlike Anne, Ms. Spencer decided to be more tactful about it.

"What are you suggesting?" I said.

She shrugged her slight shoulders. "I'm not suggesting anything, Quinn. You're in charge of your life, not me. I'm merely hoping that you take into consideration the experiences of others who have already walked the path you're on." She reached out and touched my elbow for a moment, then let her hand drop.

"Now I have a few matters of my own to attend to. So unless you have anything you'd like to say...?" Ms. Spencer said.

115

"No. I think I understand. Thank you," I replied.

She went and opened the door for me, then closed it when I left. I took a few steps down the hall and stopped, my mind still trying to process our conversation.

She knows what's been going on, I thought. Well, not everything that happened, of course. But apparently more than enough to figure things out on her own. For the first time since I finished college, I felt uncertain of what I wanted.

Or who I wanted, for that matter.

Chapter 15

VAUGHN

Is this a good idea? I wondered while I watched the dial count off the elevator floors.

I'd stayed clear of Quinn like she wanted for as long as I could. But I'd never been good at impulse control, especially not after becoming so successful.

And for the past three days I could think of nothing but her, and the way her lips tasted, the way her body fit against mine. Her resistance was maddening.

I tried not to think about her, I really did. I tried not to want her, well. However, both of those became cruel inversions. The more I pushed her from my thoughts, the more she entered them. The more I tried to forget about how she smelled, tasted, felt, the more I need to feel those things again.

How one woman could have such effects on me, I didn't know. All I knew was that she did.

I needed relief. I needed it so bad I ached. It hurt so much I came close to falling back on my old standby ways of dealing with my buried feelings. It would have been so easy to find someone to share a night with.

I hadn't, though. Somehow, I resisted. Barely. I couldn't much longer, though. I knew that.

So that was how I found myself back in downtown Boston, riding the elevator up to the floor she worked on.

"Are you…?" a young woman in business attire asked. She'd gotten on five floors ago, and I'd felt her staring at me from the corner. It was something I was used to, so it didn't bother me so much.

"Yes," I said, turning more towards her. She was a pretty thing. Petite. Unable to help myself, my mouth started tugging into one of those crooked grins women liked so much on me.

"Wow! Hey, what are you doing here?" she asked.

Do you have any idea what you're doing? I asked myself. Her question knocked me out of autopilot. "I'm meeting someone."

"I'm someone," she replied right away, grinning at her own joke. She had freckles, I saw. *Quinn has freckles. I love her freckles.*

"Yes," I said, letting my wolf's grin relax into something warmer, something friendly rather than hungry. "But not the someone I'm here to see."

"Lucky them," she replied.

I nodded and turned back towards the doors, suddenly uncomfortable in my own skin. I could trace clearly the course I took in becoming who I was. Or rather, who other people thought I should be.

When the door opened to Quinn's floor my heart lurched and my breathing quickened. *Is she at her desk?* The elevators opened onto a small lobby. I knew I had to take the hall to the right down a bit and then make a left before I could see her workspace.

I may not have looked it, but I felt like a wreck inside. All this twisting turmoil in my stomach, my mind hazy. I was glad that the new app launch was still a bit away, and that I'd managed to find someone as confident as Quinn to handle it. Because I sure couldn't, not in that state.

I took a deep breath of the air-conditioned air and started down the hall. I kept trying to think of what I might say to her. Nothing seemed good enough, though.

It all sounded so petty and empty in my head. But I knew I had to say something, anything.

I turned the corner and saw Quinn's corner desk.

There was someone seated in her chair, but it wasn't Quinn. She was blonde, and she leaned forward in the chair, squinting at the monitor.

Hot anger jetted in my stomach. *Who does she think she is?* I marched up to the desk, getting a better look at her.

118

She was pretty hot, and I could tell she knew that, too. Blouse unbuttoned to show just a little too much cleavage, a beautiful face with her already high cheekbones brought out with more makeup.

Pretty much the kind of woman I usually found myself with.

"What are you doing?" I said. I sounded angry. *What is she doing at Quinn's desk?* I felt outraged.

She didn't look up from the monitor right away. "Go away or I'll make sure you get fired."

That made me grin. "Really? Let me lay this out for you. One, I don't work here. Two, even though I don't work here, one word from me and you'll be out on your ass before lunch."

First, she blanched, then she went red in the face. Clearly someone used to getting her own way, never getting spoken to for anything. Her looks let her do whatever she wanted.

It was something I was familiar with. Probably more than she was.

"If you think I'm going to take this sort of thing from…" she said, looking up from the screen. The anger in her face melted instantly, her big, blue eyes becoming the size of saucers. She swallowed, "...Vaughn Ward."

I couldn't help feeling satisfied with her discomfort. I let her squirm a little, her eyes glancing around for some escape, some excuse.

"Yes, that's my name. You recognize me, and while I don't recognize you, I know this isn't your desk."

She got control of herself and smiled at me, full, red lips parting to reveal beautifully straight white teeth. I had to hand it to her, she had some game. I had more, though.

"Mr. Ward! I'm so happy to finally meet you. I have to say, you're even more handsome in person than in your pictures." She stood up from Quinn's desk, her body sinuous and lithe, curvy and toned in all the places I usually liked women curvy and toned.

Yet I didn't feel anything. Not a single tingle of arousal.

She strutted in front of the desk and then sat on the edge of it, letting her posture push her chest out while she crossed her legs as slowly as she could.

"You're right, this isn't my desk. It's Quinn's... I mean, Quinn Windsor. I don't mean to talk behind other people's backs, but she really hasn't been up to the task..." she leaned forward conspiratorially, her chest thrusting out even more, "She's needed a lot of help."

I crossed my arms. "And you've been helping her, I take it?"

She smiled and I knew she bought it. "Yes! That's why I'm at her computer; I was looking over some stuff for her before she sent it on to you. She's *so* incompetent."

I nodded, playing along, a hot ball of anger expanding in my stomach, "And you think you could do better? Eliminate the middleman?"

Her pretty eyes sparkled with greed. My stomach twisted at the sight. *Beauty really is only skin deep for some people, I guess.*

I wondered if that statement included me.

"Actually, yes! I know you'd be happier with me. All you have to do is talk to Mr. Callaghan. I'm sure he'll make the change right away for you. We'll do *anything* for you, here. We want to make sure you're satisfied. Fully."

She reached out and put her hand on my bicep. My stomach turned again. She looked up into my eyes, blinking slowly so that I might better see her long lashes. She even let the tip of her tongue slide out along her lips to leave them glossy and plump.

Then she looked to her right and smiled, "Quinn!"

Hearing her name, I turned as well. Quinn stood just down the hall. I saw that she'd let her hair down and I smiled.

"I was just explaining to Mr. Ward here how it would be in his best interest for him to let me take over his account," the woman said. She still had her hand on my arm.

Quinn didn't respond. She looked frozen, her eyes the only thing moving. And they moved between the woman and me.

"You haven't told me your name," I said.

She gave me another of those slow smiles, and she kept shooting triumphant looks over in Quinn's direction. I was boiling inside. I could barely contain it. "You can call me Trish if I can call you Vaughn."

"That's not going to happen," I said, "But I'm going to tell you what *is* going to happen. First, you're going to get your hand off me. Then you're going to get out of my sight and pray that I never see you again."

Trish sucked a breath in through her teeth, her eyes widening with shock. Her fingers stiff, she pulled her hand off my arm. Her anger and shock rendered her inflexible, and she lurched up from Quinn's desk.

She decided to give it one more shot, smiling at me again, her cheeks coloring. "Vaughn, Mr. Ward, you're not going to be happy with her! Me, on the other hand…"

I shook my head, silencing her. I spoke slowly so that I knew she understood. "Did anything I just said suggest that you could speak? I know what you are. I can see right through you. Now get out of here, unless you'd like to see me angry."

I left out the part about how I knew what she was because I used to be something similar. *Used to be,* I thought, looking over at Quinn. *Not anymore. Never again.*

Trish shot an angry look over at Quinn, the expression turning her face ugly. Then she left in a huff. She left quickly, too.

I breathed, trying to calm myself. Then I hooked my thumbs in my pockets and turned to Quinn. She kept looking back over her shoulder, as though she couldn't quite believe what had just happened.

"What…?" she said, caught off-guard.

I tilted my head towards her desk and computer. "I saw her sitting there looking at something on your screen. I knew it wasn't her desk, so we had a conversation about it."

"Something on my computer?" she said, looking at the device. Then her eyes went wide. "Oh!"

Chapter 16

QUINN

The picture! I thought right away. I had it saved to my desktop, the icon right there against the background for anyone to see. Anyone enough of an ass to snoop on someone else's computer. Someone like Trish.

Must not have logged off completely when Ms. Spencer called.

A million things shot through my mind. Vaughn was here. He'd met Trish. Trish had touched him, tried to work herself on him.

…And he had told her to get lost. I saw the way she'd been licking her lips and batting her eyes and thrusting her tits out at him. I remembered how I'd told him to have fun with that bartender.

In fact, for the past three days I was assuming he'd taken her home after we left that pub. But maybe he hadn't. He'd seen right through Trish's little seduction and tossed her aside.

And he's here. In front of my desk. Smiling at me. I thought right away of Ms. Spencer and her missed opportunities. Ward was my opportunity, I knew.

Ward, whose college picture was on my computer.

"So, what do you think she was doing?" Ward asked. He started around my desk, intent on finding out what snooping had been done.

I didn't want him to see that picture, didn't want him to know that I'd found it. It seemed private, somehow. Something about his past I wasn't entitled to see.

"Here, let me," I said, hustling over so fast my hair lifted up off my shoulders. *Ah, the hair!* I thought, *he must see I left it down.*

I plunked my butt down in the chair and used my body to try and hold him away. It looked like Trish had been going through some of my recent slideshows and documents.

That made my shoulders slump with relief. She probably hadn't seen the picture. If she had, she wouldn't have held that back. She wasn't that sort of person. If she had a dart to throw at you she tossed it right away.

"Everything okay? You know, I could make sure that she's not working here tomorrow," Ward said.

I considered it for a moment. It would be so delicious to get her out of here, to see the expression on her face while she cleaned out her desk and while security marched her out.

It felt too easy, though, and she deserved so much worse than that. "No, forget about it. She'll get what's coming when she's due. And no, it doesn't look like there's any permanent damage."

"No permanent damage? I like the sound of that," he said.

I glanced at him and he smiled. My cheeks started heating up so I turned back to my screen. "We'll see," I said.

I wanted to ask him what he was doing here, but I also got the compulsion to get rid of that picture before it actually did cause any trouble. I knew I should wait until later, but after having my computer snooped once while I was away I didn't want to risk it again.

I'll just drag it over to the trash bin. The thumbnail's so small, he won't know what it is.

I pretended to check a few of the files Trish had looked at. Then my moment came. Ward looked away, uninterested in what I was doing. I minimized the windows quickly and then clicked the image.

I started moving it.

"What is that?" Ward said. My heart lurched up into my throat.

"Just some old file I'm deleting," I said.

"Where did you find that?" he said. He took my hand

off the mouse and then clicked the picture again to make it full-sized. A young Vaughn Ward and his two college friends smiled out at us.

Excitement blipped inside me. I'd been so curious about that picture and the effect it might have on Ward. I thought that I must have let myself get caught there, my subconscious unwilling to deny my curiosity.

"Some old college message board," I said.

"*Why?*" Vaughn said. His tone caught me off guard. He stared wide-eyed at that picture. It looked like he couldn't decide whether he should be enraged or terrified.

"It's just some old picture," I said, my own nerves acting in sympathy with his. "You were a cute nerd back then."

"You didn't have any right to go looking for this," he said, his teeth clenched. The tendons started standing out in his neck.

"I wasn't looking for this specifically. I was just doing some research. Why are you so upset? You look happy there with your friends. Maybe a little goofy in that shirt, but certainly nothing to be embarrassed about."

I didn't know what sort of nerve I'd struck in him. Only that it was a deep one.

"Get rid of it," he said, his eyes hunting over my keyboard for the delete button.

"Yeah, sure, fine," I said. I wanted to know why he felt the way he did when he saw it. What memory did it bring back that was obviously so upsetting to him? I dragged the picture over to the recycling bin and then clicked around until that was empty, too.

"There, it's gone. You want to tell me why you came here, now?"

His eyes kept scanning my desktop, as though he didn't quite believe that the picture was really gone. I'd never seen him so unnerved and upset before. I didn't even think he was capable of those feelings.

Then again, a couple hours ago I didn't think he'd

been that kind of person in college. I had the urge to comfort him, but I wasn't certain how. I reached out for him.

He recoiled from my hand. "No. This was a mistake. You were right. Emails only."

He turned and started back towards the elevator lobby. I stood up, watching him over the false wall. "Vaughn! Wait!"

He jerked at the sound of me using his first name, but didn't stop. He continued around the corner to the elevators.

What the hell was that? I wondered. *It was just an old school picture!* And then I wanted to follow him. I looked at the clock. Not even lunch yet. I couldn't leave work. Shouldn't, rather.

I'd never skipped out on work, never left the office before it was time to go. Most of the time I stayed late.

Except work didn't seem so important at that moment. It was diminished in my mind.

I couldn't think about anything but the stricken look on Ward's face when he saw the picture. And then I recognized that expression. It was like seeing a ghost, seeing someone from the past you thought was out of your life and had suddenly reappeared.

But what could possibly haunt him so much? What could make him crack like that? I had to find out.

This time, I carefully logged off my account on the computer before leaving my desk. And then I went to catch the elevator down.

From there, I went to Vaughn Ward's brownstone.

***

I didn't know if he would answer the door, but I rang the bell anyway. My heart kept pounding in my chest, and I could feel sweat gluing my blouse to the small of my back.

126

I kept thinking about the look on his face, my curiosity over the photo, and Ms. Spencer's speech about missed opportunities.

I didn't have long to think about it, because Ward answered the door before I could even think about ringing the bell again. He'd taken the time to compose himself again, and once more he looked like the man I'd known before.

I tried picturing him with the smile I saw in that picture and couldn't. Although I also found that it did feel nice to be near him.

"What are you doing here?" he said.

"It's not obvious? I came to talk to you," I replied.

He frowned. "About the picture, I'm guessing."

"Yeah. That and other things."

He gave it some thought, and for a little bit I thought he might actually ask me to leave. The frown disappeared, his forehead smoothing out, and he stepped aside. "Come in, then."

I did. He started up the stairs, probably heading up to the third floor and its big den. I didn't want to go there, though. It made me think of Alisha and her warning, and any other women he might have had up there.

"Can we stay down here, maybe?" I said. He turned around on the stairs, another frown directed at me. He nodded, then led me to another, smaller sitting room with bare brick walls, a couch, and an easy chair.

He took the couch and I sat down in the overstuffed chair, the leather pleasantly cool for now.

"Are you going to make me drag it out of you?" I said, wanting to dispense with all the meaningless preamble. "I've been trying to figure you out since we met. What is your deal, Ward?"

Ward sat back, his hands gripping his knees, and nodded. He looked me in the eye, his gaze intense.

"That picture was taken my senior year. I was smiling because I'd just released my first app and it looked like it was promising. It was such a simple thing, but I guess sometimes the simplest things are the ones most often overlooked. I was expecting beer money, maybe something to put towards my loans after graduation.

"It exploded. I couldn't explain it, no one could. The only fact that seemed to matter was that I was suddenly pretty much a rock star. Then I had another idea, and another. And not long after that I had people working for me, my face was appearing on magazines. I had publicists getting me interviews, personal trainers getting me in shape. And I didn't know why. How could a few lines of code, code that anyone else in my class could have come up with, start up all that?"

It was my turn to frown. I leaned toward him, "You don't think you deserve any of it?"

"Maybe. Sometimes I feel like I was just in the right place at the right time, and somehow I keep ending up back there. Except now I'm not who I used to be. Now I'm who people expect me to be. And if that's true, how do I deserve any of this?"

He thinks he's an impostor, I thought. And that no one seemed to see it but him. That was what he feared, I knew: he thought that if someone was with him long enough, looked at him close enough, they might see through the façade.

It was almost funny, but not in a comic way.

"No," I said. "You are who you make yourself to be. Trust me on that one."

"And what have I made myself?" he said, spreading his hands and grimacing.

"Well, I don't know what you *think* you've made of yourself. Only what I can see of you."

"Do I want to know?" he said, smiling.

"You're the type of person who lets himself put a lot of faith in other people, but doesn't hold any back for himself. Maybe you need a bit of that faith to believe that maybe you deserve what you've made. Sure, maybe that first release was luck. Everyone needs a little luck. But everything that came after that? There's no such thing as coincidence. Especially not that many times."

He cocked an eyebrow at me, "No such thing as coincidence? Coincidences like the two of us meeting?"

Heat flushed my cheeks and I had to look down from his eyes. "Maybe."

"So what else did you want to talk about?"

"I don't know what you mean," I said.

"You told at the door that you wanted to talk about more than the picture. What is it? And don't tell me it's something to do with the account."

Now that I sat there, alone with him, I wasn't certain I could do it. I mean, I wanted to. His little reveal about his past really did push past those barriers I'd set up around me, trying to keep him out. He wasn't who I'd first thought he was.

"Nothing. I should go," I said. I stood and started for the door.

He caught me, turning me so that I faced him, pulling my body against his. "Don't tell me that. Not after what I just told you."

I swallowed, my throat dry and closing. We were so close. Our hips touched. His fingers were gentle but firm, holding me in place. I started trembling inside, heat building up in my core.

"Someone told me that I really needed to think about my life. What I want out of it… and who I want in it."

"Who do you want in it?" he said, his eyes searching back and forth between mine.

"Are you really going to make me say it?" I asked him.

He didn't. He kissed me instead, hauling my body harder against his. My hands slipped up the firm flesh of his stomach, up under his arms so that I could grab his shoulder blades and pull him even closer.

His mouth was hot on mine, and fit against me

129

perfectly.

Then, his face flushed, he pulled away. "You know what you want now? You're not going to tell me *never again*, and push me away?"

"No," I said, my lips tingled from the kiss, and I missed his mouth against mine. I gave into his desire and mine.

"Then show me," he said. We kissed again, more fiercely than even before.

He picked me up and I wrapped my legs around his waist. I looked down into his face. The air rushed in and out of my lungs like fire, but I still couldn't get enough of it.

We paused every few steps to kiss some more. I needed the feeling and the pressure of his lips against mine, and he needed it, too.

"Where are you taking me?" I asked when he carried me out of that room.

"To bed," he replied.

We started up the stairs and I tightened my legs around his waist until I realized that he had no trouble carrying me up them.

And now that I'd given myself over to my desires I couldn't wait any longer. My inner thighs burned. My clothes felt stifling and tight. And I needed to see what he looked like without anything covering him up.

His suite was on the second floor, and when he opened the door it revealed a large bed in the middle of the floor and a curtained picture window hiding us from the rest of the world.

He set me down on my feet, keeping his hands on my hips to steady me. We kissed again, and this time I put my hands between us, popping the buttons out of their loops on his shirt one at a time.

He made a deep, satisfied sound when I pulled the tails of his shirt from his pants and then put my hands on his bare, flat stomach.

His skin was warm and soft to the touch, but beneath that firm and hard.

"You like?" he said.

"God, yes," I replied. He was an Adonis, a perfectly-sculpted statue of ideal male beauty, everything in proportion, everything toned and smooth.

I kissed his neck, letting my lips slide down to his chest. The feeling of my lips against his body exhilarated him, and his strong fingers squeezed me. He ran them up into my hair, balling them into fists so that he tugged at the root.

"You're so beautiful," he said. His mouth pressed to mine again. Pressed close to his body like this, I could feel the barely-restrained passion locked within him. I wanted him to release it, to let me feel the full force of it.

His mouth slipped away from mine, running down the delicate, sensitive skin of my throat, and stopping only when the collar of my blouse got in the way.

"We have to do something about all this clothes you have on," he said. I felt his lips curl into a smile against me.

"What do you suggest?" I said. The heat in my body reached dangerous levels. I began trembling all over. Too much more of this and I thought that my skin would get hot enough to simply burn all the fabric covering me up.

Then Vaughn picked me up again, scooping me up off the floor with one strong arm under my knees and the other supporting my back. He climbed up onto the bed and set me down gently.

I could feel him trembling too. The fire in his eyes told me he wanted to tear the clothes from my body and ravish me. The restraint told me he wanted to control himself, to make this last.

I started unbuttoning my blouse, eager to take things to the next level.

He grinned. "No, you don't," he said. He grabbed my hands and then pinned both my wrists above my head against the mattress.

Then with his free hand, he continued the job I'd started. His fingers kept brushing against the bare skin of my chest. Desire and need fluctuated and shifted up and down my body. I couldn't keep still, writhing about on the mattress beneath him.

Every time his fingers grazed my bare skin I sucked a breath in through my teeth. My skin tightened into goosebumps at every caress, my breasts ached with the need for his touch, my nipples stiffening until they panged.

"Will you be gentle?" I said.

"I'll be whatever it takes to have you screaming my name," he replied, his hungry wolf's grin returning.

He undid the final button and pushed the blouse down my sides. A thread of worry moved through me. I wasn't as toned as a swimsuit model, not as tanned as a cover girl. What if he didn't like what he saw?

But then he traced his fingertips down the middle of my stomach, his touch barely grazing me but somehow still making me gasp. He let those fingers move in a gentle circle around my navel before traveling back up between my breasts to cup my cheek.

He leaned down to kiss me and I arched my head up to meet him, but he pulled back at the last second, smiling a teasing smile while I yearned for him.

"That's not fair. You're so much stronger than I am," I said, one of his hands holding my wrists firmly against the mattress, keeping me from moving any closer to him.

"I don't fight fair," he replied. He slid his other hand back down my stomach. Then between my thighs. He pressed where I wanted pressure most. My hips lifted off the mattress, trying to push him harder against me.

I wished there was nothing between us.

"I love the little sounds you make when you feel good," he said, his fingers still working their marvelous pressure between my thighs.

Then he let go of my wrists and sat on the bed beside

me. Before I even knew it happened, I found myself on his lap, the two of us kissing fiercely while we both worked to push my blouse down off my arms. His big, warm palms slid up my back, found the strap of my bra, and undid it with a single flick.

I loved the way he watched as I revealed myself to him, loved the well I felt his desire swell when I slipped the bra off.

He kissed my neck again, reveling in the freedom of movement of his lips against me, no more clothing to stop them. He slipped that hot mouth of his along my throat, my shoulders, and down between my breasts.

I put my fingers into his luxuriant hair, squeezing them into fists when he suctioned one nipple into his mouth and let his tongue lash against it until I groaned and shivered on his lap.

And then he only stopped to move over to the other one.

Then he laid me down on the bed beneath him. I ran my hands along his bare shoulders and chest, down to his abs. He was impossibly sexy and arousing. His desire rolled off him in waves.

"I'm going to make you feel better than any man has made you feel before," he said.

"Show me," I said.

"I'd rather taste you," he replied. He slid his mouth down my throat again, down between my breasts, the nipples still puckered and raw. His mouth kept going until it could go no more, meeting the waistband of my pants.

He sat up briefly, long enough to peel my pants down off my legs, and then my panties.

My heart hammered in my chest. I was completely naked before him, nothing left to hide. I forgot about all that when he put his mouth on me again, just below my navel.

It was almost too much, feeling him so close, knowing what he wanted to do to me. I could barely

133

withstand the anticipation of feeling the wet heat of his mouth slide first to the crease in my flesh where one leg met my thigh, and then over to the other.

He urged my thighs apart and then slid his mouth down between them. I kept feeling the light, delicious tickle of his stubble, the hot wash of his breaths.

"Oh, yes…" I groaned, my hips lifting up off the bed again when he put his mouth where I wanted it most. He put his hands beneath my hips and held me there against him like that, powerless to stop him.

He devoured me. Teasing at first, his kisses and his tongue grazing me. Then harder, more insistent.

Heat rushed up and down my body, so hot I thought it might burn both of us up. I reached down and grabbed onto his wrists, holding on for dear life while he coaxed and urged incredible pleasures out of me.

My whole body shook and trembled, going rigid with my climax. He guided me through it, taking me higher and higher. He was right; no man had ever made me feel this good, no man had ever been so attentive to my needs and my pleasure.

"Vaughn!" I screamed, his name ripping from my lungs.

Time lost meaning in that moment. It felt like forever and no time at all before my body relaxed and he let my hips sink back down to the bed. My eyes felt wet, and a heavy, languorous lassitude threatened to overtake me. I gulped down air, never seeming to get enough.

Vaughn slid his body up along mine, easily supporting his weight over me with those strong arms of his. He kissed and nuzzled at my neck before moving his lips up to my ear.

"Are you ready for more?" he whispered.

"There's more?" I replied. I thought I'd been satisfied. I was wrong. An aching ball of desire formed deep inside me. "Yes."

He smiled, leaning back to finally strip his shirt all the

way off. He didn't stop there, either. I'd had the idea that I wanted to tear all his clothes off with my teeth, but watching him strip down slowly was even better.

"Do you still want me to be gentle?" he asked. He grabbed some protection from the nightstand and I watched hungrily as he rolled it on.

"I want you. Hard, gentle, however I can have you," I said.

And then he rolled back on top of me. We kissed again, his curious tongue pushing my lips open and exploring my mouth.

His kiss deepened. His hardness pressed against me, then slipped inside. I grabbed his shoulder blades and dug my nails in, my snug grip around him making the both of us groan.

Again, he started off gently, pushing deeper, letting our bodies sink together, letting me get used to his size and his hardness.

And the heat, oh God, the heat, I kept thinking. How could he feel so hot inside me like that?

He continued kissing me. He kissed my mouth, my cheeks, my neck and shoulders, his lips worshiping my body.

The more I let myself fall into the experience, the better it became. I tried letting go of everything. I let go of all my earlier reservations about him. I let go of caring for nothing but work.

I let go of it all until the only thing that remained was our two bodies entwined together on his bed. I breathed in the clean smell of the perspiration he worked up. I lifted my head up so that I could kiss his jaw and feel his stubble prickle me.

I ran my hands along the planes his muscles made in his back, then traced my fingers down the tendons and veins standing out in his arms. I brought my hands back up, my fingertips bumping over his ribs.

Then I slid my hands so that I cupped that fantastic

ass of his. There was something incredibly arousing about feeling those muscles flex and relax in rhythm with his strokes.

I squeezed him and he grinned at me. Then I grabbed his ass harder and pulled him forward, both of us gasping when he sank all the way into me.

"This feels so good…" I said, closing my eyes and letting my head sink back against the mattress, exposing my neck.

Unable to resist, Vaughn kissed my throat against. He grabbed each of my hands in his, threading our fingers together, and we made them into fists. I wanted to feel him squeeze me, and I liked the weight of him pushing me down from above.

"It's even better than I'd fantasized," Vaughn said. He looked so good with the little beads of sweat on his cheeks.

"You fantasized about me?" I said, quivering around him. How could someone as hot as he was fantasize about someone like me?

"Every night," he said, "I thought about how badly I wanted to kiss you. How I wanted to run my mouth over every inch of you. I thought about how sexy you'd be with your hair spread around your head like this…" He put his face closer to mine, grazing his lips along my cheek until I could feel them against my earlobe. "And I definitely couldn't help thinking about how tightly you'd grip me."

"Vaughn…" I groaned again. I couldn't believe how he brought out the woman in me. The deeply sexual, in-tune-with-her-desires woman I normally kept locked up so tightly.

"I like it when you say my name that way," he said.

"Vaughn," I said again, my voice sounding light but actually laden with desire and need.

He sat back, still inside me, and then propped my legs against his shoulders. His thrusts took him deeper than before. *So deep!* I sucked in a breath.

The sudden an intense sensation of it made me grip handfuls of the duvet.

"Oh, God! Don't stop! Please, don't stop!" I said. The slippery heat inside me intensified. Every thrust brought me closer and closer to nirvana. He had me so close. If he stopped or slowed now I'd die. I'd just burn up into a pile of ash on his bed.

"Why stop when I can go faster?" Vaughn said.

He made good on his promise. Our bodies pressed together fast, so fast.

That tight ball of pleasure low in my stomach threatened to burst. I wanted it to explode. I wanted it so much.

My shoulders and back started lifting up off the bed. I needed him deeper, harder. And he fulfilled those needs. Oh, did he ever.

"Vaughn!" I called out again while I went over the tipping point. The tendons and muscles started standing out in his neck and shoulders, and I knew he could barely take it, either.

"Come with me. I want you to come with me," I said, reaching up and grabbing his forearms.

"Quinn…" he groaned.

We climaxed together, every muscle in my body and his contracting and pulling almost to the breaking point. I could barely stand the sensation of him flexing inside of me, and the pulsing heat that followed.

That heat worked its way into my, riding in waves up and down my body again and again until I thought I might burn up with it.

When we both relaxed, he let my legs down off his shoulders and held himself over me again, letting his lips nuzzle against my neck and shoulder.

I felt like jelly all over, every single one of my muscles so relaxed I was surprised I didn't turn into a puddle on his bed. *How can he still hold himself up like that?* I marveled at him.

"It should be illegal, how good you smell," he said, his voice somewhat muffled with his mouth so close to me.

His breath tickled and I giggled. That surprised me. I couldn't remember the last time I'd actually giggled. Laughed, yes. Chuckled? Of course. Giggling? Since when?

"I can't possibly," I said, "You've got me all sweaty and hot."

"So hot…" he agreed. He was still inside me, and I quivered around him. "Round two?"

"What? You couldn't possibly be ready that quickly!" I said, thinking he was teasing me. "Besides, I don't even think I could stand up right now even if the house caught fire around us." I wasn't even starting to get sore yet. No one could go again that quickly. Especially not a guy. They always needed more time to recharge.

I luxuriated on his bed beneath him, stretching my arms out. He liked this, kissing down to my wrist and then back up, then over to the other arm.

"Who said anything about standing up? Besides, I know you like it when I surprise you."

I looked in his eyes and saw that what we'd just done still hadn't quenched the fire of desire in them. *He's serious!* But how could he be?

"You're just teasing me," I said.

He shook his head, "I never tease about this sort of thing."

And then he went to grab more protection from the nightstand.

He was right, there wasn't any standing involved. There was a great deal of me crying out his name. And him calling out mine.

I completely lost track of time. Was it dark out? Was it past midnight? Wasn't it a work night? All questions I didn't care about.

All I cared about was the weight of his arm draped over me, the two of us lying in his big bed in the afterglow of it all.

He spooned me so nicely, his body warm and firm and comforting against my back, that I went immediately into a deep and dreamless sleep.

Chapter 17

VAUGHN

It had been two days since Quinn came to my house and dragged that confession out of me.

Two wonderful days in which neither of us stepped out of said house. Everything we could possibly want or need I ordered in.

I couldn't get enough of that body of hers. Sometimes we took it slow, going up to the bedroom and teasing each other until we couldn't take it anymore.

Other times, neither of us could contain ourselves and I would push her down onto whatever flat surface was available, pulling her hips back against me.

And thank God it's the weekend! I thought. Quinn had given into her desires, yes. But I don't think anything short of a natural disaster could have stopped her from going into the office.

The thing was, the more I saw of her the more I wanted to see. It didn't seem possible to tire of being around her.

Take this moment, for instance. I sat at the island in my kitchen. Quinn stood at the stove, trying to make what I believed to be scrambled eggs and toast for breakfast.

She kept her hair down, and I liked how glossy it looked in the morning sunlight while it bounced around her shoulders.

She wore one of my button down shirts and nothing else. A cream-colored one with a black collar. It hung down just enough to cover her butt. I could see where those lovely cheeks of hers met her thighs, and seeing that stirred the desire inside me again.

It all seemed so perfect. But even now something lurked in the back of my mind. It was an invisible countdown, I knew. Just like the ones I'd had with Stacey and Alisha and all the others.

Is it weeks? Months? I wondered. Then, *No, it's different this time. I told her things I never told anyone else. Of course it's different this time.*

The thought was enough to distract me until I smelled the distinct odor of burning toast. And, sure enough, little grey curlicues of smoke rose out of my artisanal toaster from its perch on the granite counter.

"Why is this going wrong?" Quinn said, dropping the spatula on the oven top and lifting her hands in defeat. That arm-lifting action also lifted my shirt up along her back, and the desire turned to an ache inside me.

However, I don't think either of us could answer that call just now. We were both too sore.

"Let me show you how it's done," I said, getting up off the barstool. I frowned at the burnt stuff in the skillet, which I took and washed down the disposal in the sink.

Quinn blushed. "You know, I'm normally pretty good at cooking up simple stuff like this. Just ask the kids I babysit sometimes. I don't know what happened to me."

"I happened to you," I said, grinning while I grabbed the carton of eggs from the fridge.

"You're giving yourself a lot of credit, mister," she said. She grabbed my butt through my pants and gave it a squeeze.

"No more than what's deserved. Now step back before you do to this batch whatever you did to the last."

That earned me another slap on the butt. I didn't mind. I liked that Quinn tried cooking for me. But I have to say, I got a lot of satisfaction from doing the cooking for her.

She kept shaking her head like I was so unbelievable. I wondered what sort of men she'd been with before who wouldn't do something so easy like cooking breakfast for her.

Half an hour or so later we both sat at the island, our

scrambled eggs and toast with the sides of fresh-squeezed juice and fresh-ground coffee all gone. The kitchen smelled good.

"I need you to tell me that these past few days were real. That they meant something to you," Quinn said, transfixing me with her eyes.

"Of course they meant something. You mean something to me, something important," I said.

"Because I'm not usually like this with people. I don't let this sort of thing happen, not this quickly. And I need you to know that this didn't mean nothing to me. I guess I'm trying to say that you have me in your hands now, and that you can't let me slip through your fingers."

"That's not going to happen," I said. I reached across the granite island top and took her hand in mine. I gave her a reassuring squeeze. She looked at me for a while, I suppose trying to figure out whether I meant it.

It satisfied her. "Good. I had to get that out of the way. I'm sorry if it was awkward or anything."

I had to say it did hurt a little that she felt she needed to ask those questions. However, I could also without much difficulty reason why she had asked, knowing what she did about me.

She was intelligent. She didn't jump into things lightly. She needed assurances. And after I forced myself through my first few moments of reaction I found I appreciated her more than before.

I didn't tell her about that hidden countdown I sensed at the back of my mind. With any luck, it was a countdown to nothing. A leftover from an obsolete version of myself.

"Is it Sunday?" Quinn asked.

"Yes," I replied.

"Then I should get back to my place," she said.

I didn't let go of her hand. "There's no need for that. Literally anything you could want or need, I can have here before lunch. Stay."

Her cheeks heated up, emphasizing her freckles. I loved making her blush. Those freckles had to be simultaneously the most adorable and the sexiest features I'd ever seen on a woman.

"I can't. Your marketing launch is getting so close now. Even taking this weekend off might have been too much. I haven't even checked my email, my phone's dead. Who knows what's waiting for me in the mail back home…"

She got up, pulling her hand from mine, and I could see Quinn the professional taking over for Quinn the lover.

"Forget the ad stuff for now. I'll just push it back another week," I said.

It would take my board of directors some cajoling to go along with, but since I was the majority stockholder in the company they would just have to deal with it. Right at that moment I could have happily sold Phoenix Software if it meant no one would ever bother the two of us again.

She looked at me with hope and gratitude in her eyes, and a similar hope flared in my chest. Then those lovely green eyes of hers hardened and she shook her head.

"No, no more distractions. When I start something, I finish it, and I intend on finishing this, too."

I stood and wrapped my arms around her, clasping them just below her navel. She leaned her head back against my shoulder and I breathed in the sweet, clean smell of her hair.

"Are you sure? I can be very distracting when necessary."

She reached around to the back of my head and then pulled me down so that we could kiss. She tasted sweet. Everything about her was sweet, and I couldn't stop thinking about how all she had on was my shirt.

Then she pulled away from me, spinning out of my arms like a dancer. "Not on your life," she winked.

She left before lunch after a fresh shower (which I

was forbidden from joining her in). She stepped out the door telling me that she just wanted a few days to get everything settled with the marketing push and then we could continue.

A short pause, she called it. I told her that it better be short, because I didn't know how long I could wait.

I waited until the door closed, then started thinking of the best way to surprise her. There was no way I could wait several *days* before picking up again.

Chapter 18

QUINN

I walked down the street feeling more exhilarated and alive than I'd felt in, well, ever. The breeze blowing through my hair was sweet and cool. Colors looked sharper and more vibrant. I smiled at my fellow pedestrians.

They must have thought I was a nut job. For once, I didn't care what anyone else thought.

I didn't even mind the extra couple blocks I needed to walk before finding a taxi.

I wished my phone hadn't died. I wished Vaughn would have let me at his computer for a bit. Though, there had been that one time I'd gone into his study. I'd even gotten as far as turning the computer on before Vaughn came in, folded me in his arms, and took me again, right there in that chair.

I need to know what's going on! I thought. So many distractions. The old me would have despaired at the amount of time I'd lost.

For once I went home hoping that Mary wouldn't ask me to look after the kids tonight. I needed every moment I could beg, borrow, or steal. I even thought about grabbing a few supplies and heading over to the office.

No one else would be there, it'd be perfect!

I decided against that, though. Going back and forth from there would also eat up too much time.

I got back to my place, grabbed the mail, and went up to my condo. I breathed a rather guilty sigh of relief at not having encountered Mary.

Inside, away from all prying eyes, I dropped everything for a moment just so that I could do a little happy dance.

I almost wished that Anne was here so that I could spill everything to her. Almost. *That really happened. The past few days really happened! And he wants to keep seeing me!*

Not only that, but I'd believed him when he said that this meant something to him, too. That he wasn't just going to let me slip through his fingers. We both knew more about each other, now.

It was different from anything before, for both of us.

"Okay, that's enough for now. Work. It's time for work!" I said, shaking my head, trying to force it back into a serious mindset.

Thankfully, the sky hadn't fallen. There was a request from Ms. Spencer dated yesterday asking for an update that I needed to reply to sooner rather than later. Anne had attached a few of the last minute revisions I'd requested to an email. Nothing else. That was good.

And I was happy that I hadn't gotten a cat yet. It definitely would have been forgotten over the past couple days.

Then again, if things go well I won't be needing a cat... I pushed those thoughts from my mind. One, they got in the way of thinking about work. Two, they were about a future that still didn't seem quite attainable to me.

I couldn't keep myself still, though. I kept wandering around my condo, doing a circuit from the kitchen to the living room to my office, over and over.

On one of these trips I noticed that I had a message on my answering machine. I must have overlooked it in my excitement to plug my phone in and check my email.

I hit the button to play it back.

"Hey babe, I'm in town for once and I thought we could see each other again? Maybe get a little familiar? I know we can work through some of that stuff from before. See you later."

"No," I said. *Not now. Why did he have to do this now? How did he get my number?* I'd gotten a different one when I moved into the condo.

I suppose it didn't matter how he'd gotten the

number, it only mattered that he did have it.

If there was a single person in the world I didn't want to see that day (or ever again, but especially not that day). It was him. Archer, my ex from a few years ago, before I'd started at C&M.

It had been a messy breakup, and sometimes he still got it into his head that we were a thing. Like it had all just been a mistake on my part that I'd dumped his cheating, drunk ass.

I checked the time stamp on the message. It was from this morning, around the time Vaughn and I had been sitting at his kitchen island having breakfast.

If I'd been home, I could have told him to stay away. I could have told him that I had no interest in seeing him!

Part of me knew that wasn't the way Archer operated, though. He never really cared about what I actually said, only hearing what he wanted me to say.

I got angry at Vaughn for a few heartbeats, wanting to blame him. But I knew at best he was only half to blame. It took two to do what we did. It wasn't like he'd handcuffed me to his bed.

Though wouldn't that have been something? I thought with a smile. I shook my head. *Not the time to think about that, Quinn!*

It was then I'd wished I'd gone ahead and gotten that restraining order against him.

Of course, back then he had still been poisoning my mind. I still couldn't believe I'd actually felt guilty over the whole thing, like it was my fault.

I could leave, I could go somewhere and just hide out until he stops looking. Vaughn would let me stay at his place, was my knee-jerk reaction.

I was a different person now then I was when I'd been with Archer, though. I was stronger. I was successful at my job, people respected me.

He was a ghost from my past that I decided I needed to get rid of myself, to make him stop poisoning my thoughts.

I didn't know whether I should count it as luck or misfortune that I didn't have to wait long to put myself to the test.

I sat at my desk in my home office, checking ad schedules for conflicts, when I heard the knock at my door. I'd gotten so involved in my work that I almost forgot about him.

But as soon as I heard that knock my throat squeezed shut and my stomach went cold.

I considered pretending to not be home. Let him knock as much as he wanted, let him leave.

But he'll just come back! I kept thinking. I knew Archer. I knew that once he got this into his head he wouldn't stop.

My phone sat on my desk beside my keyboard. I looked at it when Archer knocked again. I could call someone for help, but who?

Vaughn, I thought, my mind going straight to him. I could call him, get him to come over. *Maybe I won't even have to answer the door!* That would be nice, letting someone else take care of my problems.

Except that wasn't the sort of person I wanted to be. They were my problems, not anyone else's, not Vaughn's. I'd taken myself this far, made my way up the ranks at C&M faster than anyone else.

An ex-boyfriend should have been nothing at all.

But if that was the case, why did every knock at the door drive right into my head? Why did it tie my stomach in knots and leave me almost paralyzed in my chair?

Bang bang bang, came from the door, louder and more insistent. "Quinn! You in there, babe?"

I worked up every ounce of courage that I could find in myself. Which turned out to be just enough to get me to stand up from my chair. Where I found the stuff I needed to walk over to the door, I didn't know.

"Coming!" I said. My voice sounded weak, and that

made me angry at myself so I said it again, "Coming!"

He's just a selfish jackass who needs to know there's no chance of anything happening between us again.

Still, I left the chain on the door when I undid the deadbolt and pulled the door open a few inches.

"Hey, baby," Archer said, grinning down at me. He looked just about the same as I remembered. Tall, well-muscled, good-looking. Another guy I used to think looked too good for a girl like me to be with. I guess I had a type.

And it looked like he'd gotten worse over the past few years. No longer content with tight shirts as they came off the rack, he'd taken to cutting the sleeves off them.

"Don't 'baby' me, Archie. You know I don't want to see you."

His grin widened at that. "Really? Then why'd you answer the door?"

Anger and frustration mingled in a hot, unpleasant ball in my chest. "To make sure you get the message loud and clear. No misunderstandings, no confusion. Get out of here and stay away from me. I. Don't. Want. You. Do I need to spell it out?"

He tilted his head, his smile changing to the one people sometimes got when dealing with small children who were so cute when they were trying to be serious.

"Really? 'cause I think you did it because you can't stop thinking about all the things I did to that smokin' bod of yours. You want another taste. So come on, baby, open up the door."

My stomach churned. "You're right, in a way. You have left a bad taste in my mouth that I can't seem to get rid of. And the only 'bod' you were ever interested in pleasing in bed was your own. And as I recall, you always managed to please yourself so quickly."

His grin broke, then, an angry red flush coming to his cheeks and forehead. "You know I don't like it when you talk back to me, baby."

"I'm not your baby, and what you like or don't like doesn't matter to me."

Then I tried to close the door. He stuck his foot in the jamb. "I'm not leaving until you let me in."

"Then you're going to be waiting a long time."

"I could break this chain, you know. Let myself in," he shot back. I looked at the chain. Even with all my bodyweight pressed against the door, there wasn't any slack in it. I didn't like giving Archer any credit, but he was strong.

"Yes, that will make me want to take you back, you breaking into my home. You sure know your way into a woman's heart."

"You always did have a smart mouth. Let me in and I'll show you the right way to use it around a man."

What did I ever see in this guy? I wondered. Even years of hindsight couldn't answer that question. It was just one of those life choices that defied explanation. A life choice that always seemed to come back to remind me of its existence.

"You're lots of things, Archie, but a man isn't one of them," I said.

I guessed that we had reached the limits of Archer's verbal sparring ability. Because he made a sound that was half a curse and half a growl and reached one thick arm in through the door.

I jerked back from his fumbling fingers, but not before they caught at the end of my hair. They tightened around the strands and then pulled.

It was a good thing he'd just gotten the ends. It hurt for a moment and then his fingers slipped off.

Now my heart really pounded inside me. My adrenaline kicked in, leaving me cold and shaky.

And then I realized I was stuck there. My home phone was in the living room. My cell was still on my desk beside my keyboard. I wished that I'd called Vaughn.

Now it was a waiting game. Either Archer would get

bored or frustrated and leave, or that chain on my door would give way.

I could hope that maybe a neighbor would come out and see the commotion and call the cops, but that one seemed the most distant hope.

"I'll scream!" I said.

"You think I give a damn?" he replied. He made another blind swipe with his hand.

Chapter 19

VAUGHN

I pulled up to the curb and grabbed my cell from the passenger seat where I'd tossed it before.

I frowned at it. Quinn still hadn't returned any of my texts or calls.

She's probably just shutting everything out so that she can get some work done, I told myself. I admired her dedication to her work, how she threw everything she had at it. I did something similar when I was working on a new project as well.

Most people found that surprising. I was the CEO of a major company that now had thousands of employees. Why do any of that menial work myself?

I always told the interviewers that I wanted my employees to respect me, not just consider me some aloof executive who reaped all the rewards from their work. That was only partly true.

I also did it because it reminded me of those simpler days, before all this success. When the most difficult thing in life was hunting down a programming bug.

Except now the only thing I wanted to do was get through this product launch and then take Quinn, who would not have that work excuse anymore, somewhere nice. Somewhere with sandy beaches and crystal waters.

Somewhere we could really just be alone and get to know each other. I found I wanted to know everything about her.

She'd resist at first, I knew. But she'd give in. I'd already come up with a few things to wear down that resistance.

Like going to her place to surprise her with lunch. I'd gotten a few looks at the grocery store loading the brown bag into this car.

I also just wanted to see her again. I felt like a different person around her, especially after sharing more about myself with her. It was almost enough to push that stupid, almost invisible countdown from the back of my mind. *That's not going to happen. Not this time.*

Parking was free on Sundays, I noticed when I got out. That was good, because small change was something that hadn't existed for me in quite some time.

I grabbed the bag out of the trunk and went into her building. Here I also felt some relief. These new condo buildings always had a secure entrance, and I wasn't certain how to get into the place without buzzing her.

But someone had propped the inner door open. Serendipity, I guess. Inside it was quiet, and I figured everyone was out enjoying the nice Sunday weather.

I got into the elevator and, shifting the brown bag to one hand, hit the button for Quinn's floor.

The elevator opened and I stepped out.

"Open the door, Quinn!"

"Just go away!" I heard Quinn say back.

Some asshole had his shoulder pressed against Quinn's door, his foot shoved into the jamb, one arm flailing around on the other side. He was big, his face all red.

I didn't say anything. My instincts pushed me past that right away. I dropped the bag and started walking. Something red and hot and dangerous ignited in my chest.

What the hell does he think he's doing?

Whatever it he thought it was, it was a mistake. A big one.

"God damn it, Quinn! I'm going to break this down in five seconds if you don't let me in!"

He pulled his arm out of the door so that he could move his body back farther to get a little bit more momentum into his shoulder.

I grabbed his shoulder and turned him to face me.

His eyes went wide when he saw me, and he started trying to say something, but I didn't give him the chance.

I cold-cocked him right in the jaw. The impact sent a shock right up to my shoulder. I had so much adrenaline pumping through me that I didn't feel anything but that shock.

His eyes rolled up into his head and head slumped against the door frame. *Glass jaw*, I thought. A bright, hot bruise already stood out on the side of his face.

I stood over him, the pain a distant throb in my knuckles that started getting closer. I lifted my hand up to inspect it and saw that a similar bruise had blossomed across my knuckles.

Part of me wished that he hadn't fallen so quickly. That desire to hurt him still burned hot in my chest, and I could feel my lips peeled back into a snarl.

The chain holding Quinn's door shut jangled when she released it. She opened the door and her eyes went wide when she looked down at the limp man leaning against her door frame.

"What happened?" she said.

I got the sudden image of this jackass trying to hurt her and my anger flared up again.

I shrugged. The ache in my knuckles kept getting hotter and sharper. "I saw him trying to get in and something just came over me."

"What are you even doing here?"

"I came to surprise you... Surprise, I guess?"

The guy on the floor started waking up. He groaned, his eyes opening one at a time. One hand went up to probe at his jaw and when he touched the bruise he hissed.

Then a door opened down the hall and a middle-aged guy poked his head out. "Everything all right? I can call the cops if you want?"

"It's fine," Quinn said. She kept looking down at the man and then up at me. I could tell she was trying to decide whether to thank me for intervening or demand to

157

know just what the hell it was I thought I was doing.

She was one of those types, I knew, who would tell me that she had it all under control. She liked having everything under control, or at least thinking she did.

All I really cared about was that she was okay.

The mention of the cops really perked the guy up. His eyes opened wide. "Cops?" he muttered. Panic flashed across his face. Panic that turned to pain when the expression pulled at his bruise. I can't say I didn't feel satisfied.

He got to his feet in a clumsy, drunken way, his hand clutched to his face, and then staggered down the hall towards the stairs. Quinn and I stood out of his way. I was happy that he didn't want to put up more of a fight, but I wouldn't have shied away if he had. I had a second fist to break on his face, after all.

It was then I saw the bag of groceries I'd dropped. Everything had broken or spilled. I groaned in disappointment.

"Vaughn…" Quinn started.

I held up my hand and she quieted. "Don't tell me you had that under control. Because you didn't."

Her face held some mixture of anger and fright, and she kept glancing down the hall as to make sure that he'd really gone.

"That's him, isn't it?" I said.

"That's who?" she said, her eyes turning to me. They looked wetter than usual.

"He's the guy that hurt you. The one that makes it difficult for you to get close to someone."

She turned her eyes down. "I don't know what you're talking about."

"Give me a break. You don't think I can recognize when someone's hiding something? I told you something about me that I never share with anyone. The least you could do is pay me that same respect."

She started looking up at me, but then she saw my

hand. "Your knuckles!"

"It's fine. Forget about it," I said, my irritation that she was still holding back on me drowning out the fiery throb slowly working its way up my wrist.

She took my hand in hers and held it up. "When something turns purple like this, it isn't fine. Come inside, I have a bag of peas in the freezer."

"That guy had a really hard head," I said. It had been like slamming my fist into a brick wall. Not that I regretted it.

"You have no idea. Come inside. Here, how's this?" she asked, pulling the bag of frozen peas from the freezer, wrapping it in a dish towel and then putting that against my knuckles.

The pressure of it hurt at first, but then the coolness soaked in. "Nice. Thanks."

She had me put my other hand over it to keep it in place and then she went and leaned against the opposite counter. She crossed her arms. I could see her shaking a little, the aftershocks of her adrenaline taking their course on her body.

I got the sense she wanted me to say something. Something sentimental or melodramatic. Something she could yell at me for being *that guy* who thought women needed saving or something.

I didn't, because I knew she wanted to use it as an excuse to not open up to me. I adjusted the bag on my knuckles so that a fresh cold spot touched them.

Finally she breathed deeply and then blew her cheeks out in a sigh. She brushed some hair out of her eyes and looked at me. "His name's Archer. We dated a few years ago, after I finished college but before I started working at C&M. He… wasn't good to me, but I didn't know any better and he kept telling me that I wasn't good enough for anyone else. He drank a lot and I knew he was cheating on me all the time."

I wanted to say something but didn't. I knew she

159

needed to get this off her chest. I also wanted to go find Archer and give him a few more bruises to match the one he had already.

Quinn started chewing on her thumb nail, a nervous gesture I'd never seen from her before. She realized what she was doing and forced her hand away from her mouth.

"I started getting my life together, though. I had interviews coming up. I made myself realize that he was the problem, not me. I broke it off and he didn't like that. I thought he'd moved on by now but I guess not."

"He will now," I said. If what I'd done hadn't deterred him, I had a team of lawyers on standby. They usually dealt with copyright stuff and other corporate issues, but I was sure that for what I paid them they could take care of Archer, too.

I didn't tell Quinn that, though. I knew she'd have none of it. I admired her obstinacy, but that didn't mean I had to obey it.

"I hope so. How's your hand?"

Chapter 20

QUINN

I wanted to yell at him. I wanted to rush into his arms and pull his face down to mine and kiss him until he begged for mercy. I didn't know which to do.

He lifted the now semi-frozen bag of peas from his hand and held it up. There was an awful bruise still spreading across his knuckles. He flexed it into a fist and then shook it out.

"It will be fine soon enough," he said.

I'd never told anyone about Archer before. He was from a different part of my life, a chapter ended and relegated to the past. I'd never even mentioned him to Anne or Mary.

I still wanted to tell him that he didn't need to do that for me. But then I kept thinking about how badly I wished I'd called him when it was happening. Someone more spiritual than I was might have called this an act of destiny.

I kept looking at him, waiting for him to say I was being silly, or to patronize me. He nodded instead, acknowledging what I said, acknowledging that sometimes that was all you could do when someone opened themselves up to another person.

I was vulnerable and he didn't take advantage of that. Like Archer had before.

And I also had to admit that while I was a modern woman who could take care of herself, there was something undeniably sexy about a man not afraid to break some knuckles in my defense.

"So… this is my condo," I said, trying a smile on. "I know it has nothing on a brownstone in Back Bay… but I like it."

He glanced around. "It's nice, really. Now I really

wish I hadn't dropped that bag."

"Come on, I'll give you the tour." I took his good hand and started leading him around, pointing out the okay view I had. I showed him my degree, framed on the wall. I lead him down the hall. "And this is the bedroom."

"Normally my favorite room of any home," Vaughn said.

Something dropped to the floor. I looked down and saw the bag of peas wrapped in its dishcloth on the laminate. It had split open at one corner and a couple peas had rolled out.

"Hey..." I started.

He stopped me with a kiss, pulling my body hard against his. My desire flared, so hot it was almost painful. I couldn't contain myself any longer. "What can I do to make you forget about that hand?" I said, kissing his chin, running my lips along his jaw.

He grinned at me. I grabbed his shirt and pulled him down for another kiss, then used that hold to back us both up into my bedroom. The back of my knees hit the mattress.

We tumbled over onto it. We couldn't keep our hands still. I groaned beneath him while he ran his hands all over me, squeezing and touching. It didn't take those fingers long to start on the buttons of my blouse.

I could see him wincing when he used his bruised hand. "Don't hurt yourself."

"I don't care about that," he said. "You're worth more than a little pain. I'll pay this and more."

He was true to his word, using both hands to tear every stitch of clothing off me as quickly as he could. My heart quickened again, my skin flushing with heat.

"You haven't had enough excitement for one day?" I asked.

He shook his head. Before I could say anything else, he sealed my lips with his. And then his hand slipped down between my thighs. I sucked in a sharp breath, pulling the air from his lungs into mine.

He didn't let me calm down, either. He touched and stroked and teased me until I was nothing but an aching ball of desire beneath him.

"How do you do this to me?" I said.

"I've been asking myself a similar question about you a lot, lately" he said. He took a moment to pull my bottom lip between his teeth and then let it slide out slowly. It left my lip plumped and throbbing for more.

"And what answer have you come up with?" I asked, sending my hand down his body. It wasn't fair that he could use his hand on me to such effect.

He liked the way I touched him. I liked that he liked that.

"The only answer I've been able to come up with is that I can't get enough of you. Every taste makes me want more."

His next touch sent an incredible bolt of pleasure up through me and I groaned beneath him. And then I couldn't stand the fact that I was naked and he was still fully clothed.

We sat up on the bed. I went behind him and pulled his jacket off. Then I undid his shirt and pulled it up out of his slacks. I pulled it partway down his back, exposing his shoulders and keeping his arms together.

Then I kissed one shoulder, letting the lines of his body carry my mouth up to his neck.

He was just as sexy from the back as from the front, too.

"Do you like that?" I whispered into his ear.

"I don't think I like anything as much as I like the way you touch me."

"How do you always know the right thing to say?" I asked. I let my lips travel back down his neck, going across to the other shoulder. Then I pulled his shirt all the way off. I ran my hands down the muscles on either side of his spine that tapered down at his waist to form a V.

Then I stepped off the bed and went around so that I could tug his slacks and his boxers off. The sight of his desire inflamed my own desire. I climbed up on top of him, pinning his hardness between us. I ached to feel him inside of me.

He grabbed me and held me close, his hands sliding down my back to cup and squeeze my ass. I loved the pressure, the barely contained need, in the strength of his fingers.

"It's not fair to be as sexy as you are," I said, biting down on his lip again.

"I'm all yours," he replied, one hand sliding up to the back of my head so that he could pull my mouth against his. We kissed savagely, we were so hungry for each other.

Then I couldn't take it anymore. I couldn't take the waiting, couldn't take the pulsing of my desire inside me.

I shifted my body along his.

"Don't we need...?" he started, his hands already moving up my stomach to cup my breasts.

"I'm on birth control, Vaughn," I said. "The only thing I need is you."

That aroused him even more, just like I thought it would. I lifted my hips, felt him against me. I sank down onto him, sucking a breath in through my teeth at how good it felt.

Vaughn's lips peeled back from his teeth and he pressed his head back against the mattress, his eyes closing.

It was even better than I thought it would be, having nothing between us at all. My body knew just what to do, rising up along him and then sliding back down.

We went slowly at first, getting used to the touch of each other. It was familiar, but different. He was familiar, now. How could he not be, after those nights I'd spent with him?

But he was right. I couldn't get enough of him, just like he couldn't get enough of me.

He squeezed my breasts, pinching my sensitive and

puckered nipples between his fingers until I gasped. Then his hands slid down to my waist, then down to my hips. He urged me to go faster, to lift myself up on him and then drop down so that our bodies slammed together.

The friction, the heat, the slickness of it penetrated right through me. I couldn't take it for long.

I let myself drop down again, burying him all the way into me as my climax seized my body and my already snug grip tightened even more.

He gasped at the sensation. I leaned down over him and he hugged me close, anchoring him to me while my orgasm threatened to carry my away.

I calmed down to the feeling of his kisses on my face. He didn't give me any chance to recover, however. No, he rolled us over so that he was on top and we started again.

I watched his abs squeeze and relax with his motions, watched the way his pleasures contorted his handsome face.

He finished inside of me, the heat of it more intense than anything I'd felt before with him.

Both of us were drained. After, we lay together on my bed. I didn't even have the sheet pulled up to cover myself, it felt so natural and normal to be around him.

Sweat glistened on both our bodies. He had his arms clasped behind his head, the pose emphasizing the sculpted muscles in his arms and chest. I rolled onto my side so that I could lay my head against that chest. I put my hand beside me and felt the rhythm of his heart.

"I wanted to get a lot of work done today," I said.

"And you got to do something else so much better, instead," Vaughn replied.

Maybe it was just the afterglow of our passion. Maybe his fending off Archer affected me more deeply than I thought it did. Whatever it was, I felt more drawn to Vaughn than ever before.

He continued looking up at the ceiling, and I looked at him, taking in his handsome profile. The strong jaw, the defined cheekbones, the clarity of his eyes.

How could I resist all of that? The answer was that I couldn't. I hadn't really given myself completely to anyone since I'd first started off with Archer. And after Archer I don't think anyone could blame me for being more guarded with my feelings.

"What are you thinking right now?" I asked.

He looked at me, his face so close to mine that I could have kissed him. I almost did, but I didn't want to interrupt him.

"I'm thinking about how nice this feels. I'm thinking about how I wish I could make these moments last forever, and I'm a little sad that despite everything that I have, I can't make that happen."

"So… you want to make this last? You and me?" I said.

"Yeah, I do," he said, nodding.

I put my hand against his cheek and kissed him, the smile on my face somewhat spoiling it.

He frowned for a moment, his lips compressing. His eyes searched around my bedroom but didn't find what they were looking for.

"What is it?" I asked, an irrational and cold fear snaking its way through my chest. I couldn't help my first thought being that he was about to tell me that this had all been for fun. That it was good while it lasted but now he had other things, other women, to get onto.

I had the urge to pull the sheet up and cover myself. He turned onto his side and looked at me, his eyes boring into mine, still searching. *But for what?*

"I've been thinking about asking you something," he said.

"If it's about your account then I'd have to say that any delays there are your fault, mister."

He smiled and shook his head. That smile helped calm me down a little. "It's not about the account. Well, sort of. More about what happens after all the ads have been brought online and there's nothing left to do for a while."

"If you're asking if I'll still be in charge of your account after all that initial stuff, yes, of course! However, I think that I may have something of a conflict of interest here…" I said, putting my hand on his chest. His heart was beating faster than before.

Mine picked up in sympathy. *What is he getting at?* I admitted that I hadn't known Vaughn all that long, but I thought I knew him well enough to consider him a person who hated beating around the bush.

"I want us to go away together after all the dotting of the I's and crossing of the T's has been completed," he said. He reached up and put his hand over mine. His palm was warm again my knuckles.

"Away? Like as in a vacation? Where?"

"There's this island I own…"

"Of course you do," I said, unable to resist.

He plowed on through the interruption, "…That I think would be perfect. Just the two of us, the beach and the sun."

"But who will get me all the little drinks with umbrellas in them?" I teased.

"Yours truly. If you think I made some mean eggs then you really should try my margaritas."

I started tingling all over at the thought of spending all that time with him. It wasn't just an idle offer made to impress me, either. His eyes kept flicking between mine, checking for signs of my acceptance or refusal.

"Okay. Let's do it," I said, smiling. He kissed that smile off my face, and then we couldn't keep our hands off each other for the next few hours. This was going so well it all felt like some wonderful dream. A dream I hoped I'd never wake up from.

167

Chapter 21

VAUGHN

Two weeks went by and I didn't know how either of us managed to get any work done.

Still, somewhere in there Quinn and I managed to eke out enough time for her to finish off with the marketing push with C&M and for me to get all the final prep done at my end.

It involved two nights apart where I had to run to New York. Even in this day and age of the internet, I found it best to do some things in person. This took some pressure off my board of directors as well, who'd been trying to contact me with increasing urgency and panic.

Those two nights away were repaid with two more days and nights in my brownstone in Back Bay where neither of us went outside. Or bothered to put any clothes on, really.

Some part of me wondered if the closer I got to Quinn and the more I learned about her, the more likely it was that I might find something to make me push her away. Nothing like that happened at all.

Sometimes I felt like that part of me *wanted* to find something not to like, and I didn't know why.

There had been one thing. She told me one night that she couldn't go out, that she needed to babysit a couple kids for her friend. For a moment, I got jealous, then realized how foolish it sounded. A single mother needed all the help she could get, and I couldn't help but admire her even more for it.

And I could feel her getting closer to me, too. She laughed at all my college stories, and laughed even harder at my corporate ones (her favorite was one I liked to call "The Many Wigs of Donald Trump").

Every now and then something inside me pushed out at this comfort and closeness I felt with her. But so far I'd been successful at pushing back when I felt that.

That countdown in the back of my mind seemed to have receded into wherever forgotten memories went.

And tomorrow we would be going down in the jet to my island. We hadn't set a specified time, either. That bugged Quinn, who wanted to tell her bosses at C&M something solid.

But I just told her that as long as she was in charge of my account they would give her as much vacation time as she asked for.

A couple weeks, at least, I thought, smiling in anticipation.

"What are you smiling about?" Quinn said.

We'd just gotten back to the brownstone after a big press junket where I officially announced the release of Phoenix Software's new app. We both sat on my couch up on the third floor, the setting sun sending some rays of golden light in against the bare brick wall on the other side of the room.

"I was smiling about going away tomorrow. Getting you all to myself for all those days and nights," I said.

Quinn relaxed on the couch, her eyes closed and her head back against the cushion. She didn't have to do any speaking at the junket, of course. But she'd been in anxious knots over the first official screenings of her ads.

It had gone well, of course. She was good at her job. That junior partner position was hers any time she wanted it, from what I understood.

She made a satisfied sound in her throat. "That sounds *so* nice right now."

That sound sent tingles through my body. Electric ones that set my heart pumping. I took in the way her hair fell around her head, the way her lips parted slightly when she sighed.

I couldn't help myself. I wrapped my arms around

170

her and pulled her onto my lap so that she faced me. This close, I could smell her. That made me want her more.

"You are insatiable!" she said, smiling, her eyes glinting.

"Are you saying that you aren't? I thought you found me hot and irresistible?"

"I do. It's just that you still surprise me with it."

I put my hands on her hips and squeezed, just enough so that she knew I meant business. "I like surprising you."

"So you say." She wet her lips. Her body pushed against mine, coming into sync.

"Come here and kiss me," I replied.

She did. She put her hands on my chest, pushing her fingernails into my pectorals. I'd found myself thinking over the past little while that sometimes the kissing was so good we didn't actually need to go any further.

Of course, I always went further. But it was a thought.

It was the kind of kissing that left both of us breathless, left our mouths throbbing and raw from the force of it.

She pulled back from me, and I took the opportunity to start on the top buttons of her blouse. I wanted to reveal every inch of her skin nice and slow. Give her a good tease. The purple bruise across my knuckles had mostly faded by now, I saw. And there had been no more trouble from Archer.

Then she took my hands in hers, halting my progress. "What?" I asked, giving her fingers a gentle but insistent squeeze.

"Did you know that it's been more than a month since we met?"

"Really?" I said. Then I grinned, "Ah, yes. The hotel. You couldn't keep your eyes off me. I remember that."

Her eyebrows climbed up her forehead, "Excuse me? You were in your underwear! I tried looking everywhere *but* at you. You're the one who insisted that I come in and wait for you to shower and get ready."

I shrugged and this earned me a playful slap on the shoulder. "Don't deny it. You wanted me right away."

"I think you're confusing me with yourself, mister *'What would you do if I kissed you right now?'*"

"Oh, yeah…" I said, nodding. Then I used her hold on my hands to pull her close and kiss her again. She giggled and pulled back once more. I loved it when she giggled. The sound went so well with those freckles on her cheeks.

"You keep distracting me!" she said, wrinkling her nose at me.

"Okay, fine, I promise I won't…" Then I pulled her in for another kiss. This time I got my hands free and I grabbed her at the small of the back, pushing her hips down against mine.

I almost had her there, too. I could feel her melting against me, ready to give in. But then—and I have no idea where she got the willpower from—she pushed away from me again.

"Let me finish," she said.

I held my hands up, then shoved them down between my back and the couch. I nodded at her.

She put her hands on my chest and then slid them up to my shoulders. She sighed once, then twice.

I smiled at her. "What is it?" *What could possibly be so difficult for her to say?*

Whatever it was, my heart started thumping. My smile started to falter, but I forced it back into place.

"This sort of thing is difficult for me to say. It's that whole being protective of my feelings thing…" Quinn started. She straightened the collar of my shirt as though it were the most important task in the world. Then she looked me in the eye.

She continued. "It's been more than a month now, like I said. And we've been spending a lot of time together. And since we started all this, I've learned a lot about

172

myself. And…" her eyes fell down again.

"And, what?" I said. Pressure started in the small of my back. I realized that I had clenched all those muscles.

"*And*, I really do want to go with you tomorrow. Because I'm pretty sure that I'm falling for you." She blinked a lot and bit her bottom lip. I knew that had been difficult for her to say.

She kept looking at me, waiting for me to respond. I knew that I should. I knew I needed to.

A cold and nervous feeling swam in the pit of my stomach. I pulled my hands out from behind me and let them spread out on the couch cushions.

"Vaughn?" she said, her fingers pushing against my chest.

I swallowed and found that I could look anywhere but at her. That damn countdown in my head finally revealed itself. It hadn't disappeared like I thought it might have. And it had reached zero.

"You do know what I just told you, right?" Quinn said. Her body began going rigid. Her eyes searched my face with more and more desperation.

It tore me up inside, and I still couldn't face it. "I know."

"I'm glad you know. Do you feel the same way, maybe? When someone reveals that sort of thing, they're usually hoping for a bit of reciprocation."

"I… don't know," I said, the words ringing in my ears. I felt disconnected from myself. Like I was watching all this from somewhere just above our heads, screaming down to stop being such a fool.

Quinn climbed off my lap. She paced between the couch and the wingback chair. "How can you not know how you feel?" she asked, stopping in front of me, her hands held out, palms up.

Something about her attitude irritated me and I let that irritation seep into my voice. "I like you. You know that. I know that. Can't we just leave it at that for now?"

She crossed her arms and her jaw started working. I wanted to take back what I said, but couldn't.

"I can't believe you. You *know* that things like that aren't easy for me to say. I know you feel the same way about me, Vaughn. Can't you just admit that?"

Just the thought of saying what she wanted me to say, letting myself feel what she wanted me to feel, twisted me up inside. My hands squeezed into fists against the cushions. I looked up at her and shook my head.

"This is all a part of that impostor stuff from before," she continued. "I thought you'd moved past that. Can't you see that you do deserve your success? That it all didn't happen by accident? People aren't going to suddenly realize you're a fraud one day, because you aren't."

"Don't you think if it was that easy I would have done it already?" I snapped, once more immediately regretting the tone in my voice. I could tell I was hurting her. I wanted to stop, but I couldn't. "Things were going great the way they were. Let's go back to that."

Quinn turned away from me, one arm still clutched around her ribs, the other covering her mouth as though to try and keep any sobs from coming out. Her shoulders hunched.

"Quinn…" I said. I reached up and touched her elbow and she recoiled.

"Why do you push everyone away?" she said, her voice muffled by her hand.

I slumped back against the couch. "Because it's easier that way."

We stayed like that for a long time, her standing there facing away from me, me sitting on the couch, waiting for her to say something. I wished so desperately that I could rewind things. Go back just a few minutes.

I could feel inside that we'd crossed some invisible point where I couldn't just take everything back.

Besides, even if there was a way to turn back the clock I would probably say the same things.

"Quinn," I said again, unable to bear the waiting any longer.

"Stop talking. Just stop talking," she said. From where I sat, I could see how her face had flushed and how she trembled just a little. And how she tried to hide all that from me.

The silence pushed in on me, tension laden in the air. It was strange to think that just a few minutes earlier we'd been on the verge of making love. That moment seemed years distant, then.

"I think you should go by yourself tomorrow," Quinn said, so quiet that even in the previous silence I had trouble making out the words. I had no trouble understanding their meaning, however.

"I don't want to go without you," I said. I stood up, meaning to hold her. She stepped back from me, flinching like some animal too often abused by its master. That stung inside.

"Then I guess you're going to be disappointed. I'm leaving now, Vaughn," she said. She started towards the stairs, making sure to keep the chair between us as she went.

"Don't go," I said.

"Too late," she replied.

"Can I see you later? Can we talk?" I said. I could feel her slipping away and I didn't know how to pull her back.

She stopped at the top of the stairs, her hand on the banister. She still wouldn't turn around to look at me. "I don't know, Vaughn. I just don't know."

Chapter 22

QUINN

I sat at my desk in the C&M office. I looked at my monitor, but didn't see it. My eyes refused to focus. My fingers hovered over the keyboard, but I couldn't bring myself to tap any words out.

How could he do that?

I was a husk. Empty and singed on the inside, devoid of anything but a sort of constant, low-grade anger.

I couldn't stop thinking about Stacey and Alisha, about the way they'd both looked at me. For so long I'd thought they were looks of dismissal and disregard. But I realized now that they were actually looks of pity.

They knew about him. They knew how he plays with other people's hearts. And they knew what he would do to me, because he did it to them.

I guess somewhere I knew that. Especially after Ward's confession about his feelings. I guess that I thought that I was different, somehow. That I could and did fix him.

But who was I kidding? I wasn't a swimsuit model or an actress, rich and famous. If he could do that sort of thing to those types of women, how could I possibly think that I could? I was just an office worker. Nothing special about me.

I wanted to scream. I wanted to sweep my keyboard and my monitor off my desk and then use my chair to smash them into little bits. I didn't know who I was more angry with: Ward for doing that to me, or me for being willing to give myself to someone like that.

It wasn't a good time for Trish to show up. She'd been a sore loser ever since Ward told her what she was and where to go. I guess she somehow sensed that I was vulnerable and that he wasn't around to protect me.

She was like a shark, attracted by the smell of blood in the water.

And that made me sneer. *Protect me? The only thing he's interested in guarding are his own feelings.*

"So," Trish said, leaning up against the false wall, "I guess you're moving up in the world. No accounting for good taste, I suppose."

"Not right now, Trish," I said, giving politeness one shot. Even that required a Herculean effort on my part.

It made her raise her eyebrows in mock shock. "Not right now? I guess you have an even bigger ego than I thought you did."

That low-grade anger smoldering inside me flared up into outright rage, suffusing every muscle in my body with trembling heat. I stood up. Then I grabbed my keyboard and slammed it down on my desk hard enough for a few of the keys to pop out.

Trish's eyes widened for a second before she brought herself back under control and pasted a haughty smile to her lips. "What? Junior partner not good enough for you or something? I know, maybe your rich jerk boyfriend told you he wants you to start going to the gym. Not a bad request, if you ask me."

It was the type of anger that brought tears to my eyes. I looked at her slightly blurry face. "What is your problem? I've tried being nice to you. I've tried helping you. I've always *tried* to be polite to you…"

"Hey, I'm not the one with the problem…" she started.

"Keep your mouth shut for once. Women like you are what makes it hard to get people to respect us in the office. You are your own worst enemy. You want to know why they give all the important jobs to me? Because they know I could get them done! All they want from you is what you're oh-so-willing to give. And they don't respect you for it. They laugh about you, Trish. *You're a joke.* But for some reason the punch line always goes over your head. And that's sad. You are sad and I pity you."

I was yelling by the end of it, my shoulders heaving and my whole body hot. The rest of the floor had gone silent, and I could feel people watching me from their cubicles.

Trish's face went from red to white. She looked around and saw everyone looking at us.

"What? Nothing to say for once?" I said.

And then she shocked me again by turning and walking away. Around then I noticed the people watching me and their looks began working their way through my anger, making me realize what I just did.

"Whoa, that was pretty intense. I didn't think it was possible for that much blood to drain from Trish's face. What's wrong? Did something happen?" Anne said, making me jump.

"How long have you been standing there?" I asked.

"Since, *Women like you…*' Pretty crazy, by the way. Do you want to go somewhere so that we can talk?" she said.

The anger banked itself inside me, cooling to embers. And then the self-conscious embarrassment began. "That might be nice."

Before we could go the phone on my desk rang. I picked up, spoke for a few moments, and then put it back down. "Sorry, Ms. Spencer wants to see me right away."

Anne sucked a breath in through her teeth, giving me a commiserating look. "Good luck."

I started up to her office. She hadn't said why she wanted to speak to me, only that she wanted me up there right away. There was no way she'd heard about my little blowup already, was there?

I knocked on her door.

"Come in," she said.

It went inside just as she finished up another phone conversation and hung up the receiver.

"I was calling you up here to congratulate you in person for the way you've handled the Ward account. I've been getting some statistics. Nielsen ratings, online ad views from a few sites. Not a lot. But enough to say that we think it will be a success."

"That's good," I said, not sure what else to say.

She looked at me over the rims of her glasses. "However, I just spoke with a manager from your floor. Apparently there's been a... scene between you and another employee?"

Excuses welled up inside me. *She started it; I've been under lots of pressure lately; I let my feelings get the better of me; I pretty much told my boyfriend I love him and he told me he wants to go back to the way things were before I said that.*

I didn't say any of those, though. "There was. I have no excuse for it, but I do regret it."

Ms. Spencer nodded. "Good, because I don't want to give you the speech about office etiquette, and how that's not the type of behavior we expect from our newest, and youngest ever, junior partner. Plus, from what I've heard of this specific *employee*, she deserved every word of it."

I nodded. *She might have deserved it, but that doesn't mean it was right for me to scream at her like that in front of everyone.*

"I'm glad you understand. And now that the congratulations and the disciplining are out of the way, I wanted to see how you are doing."

"I tried to follow your advice about not letting work consume me. But I think I made a mistake," I said.

"Oh? I know it's not my business, but from what I've seen things have been going quite well between the two of you."

"I don't think things are going to work out between us. But don't worry, I'll make sure it doesn't affect my work any more than it already has. I fully intend to live up to everyone's expectations of me here."

"Don't be silly," Ms. Spencer said. "I know that feeling, too. That desire to throw yourself into something

180

to get away from something else. It's none of my business, like I said, and you're free to disregard my advice. All I'm suggesting is that you don't walk away from anything lightly. Sometimes you have to jump a few hurdles before you get to the finish line."

"I'll take that under advisement," I replied, my back stiffening. I knew she was just trying to be helpful, but I didn't want any advice right then, "Is there anything else?"

"That's all."

Chapter 23

VAUGHN

I wanted so badly to the let the old Vaughn Ward reassert himself. To shrug off Quinn as just another of my long string of failed relationships. There were plenty of beautiful and willing women out there, I knew.

I could walk over to that pub on the corner and see if that redhead was behind the bar again. I could go to a party tonight.

The pain would be over. I'd shift my attentions over to someone else. Quinn would just be something of a painful memory like all the others.

I sat on the stoop of my brownstone, watching the pedestrians and the cars go by. I got a few strange looks, and I knew that people recognized me. I didn't care what they thought.

I kept looking at my car, and I kept squeezing my keys in my hand. It was after five. Quinn would be home. I could go over to her condo, try to talk to her, try to explain things.

Because she was different from all the others. And I knew I couldn't let her slip away from me like I'd done before. I couldn't make it that easy on myself.

I could call, I thought, feeling the lump of my cell phone in my jacket. *She won't answer*. I knew.

But what good would going over do? Wouldn't that make me no better than Archer, alternating between screaming at her and begging for her to let me inside?

I could tell how much I'd hurt her. I knew that she had really opened up to me, really showed me her inner self. And I'd turned her down.

Just thinking about the things I'd said to her made my blood boil. *Go back to before you said that? Are you kidding me?*

I was a wreck. I had so much baggage I didn't know how I managed to function at all. *Maybe it would be better if I just left her alone?*

I recognized that voice as the one wanting me to return to who I used to be. I wasn't going to give in. I wasn't going to give up. Not on Quinn.

I bounced my keys against my palm and then squeezed my fingers around them. Before I could second guess myself I forced myself into the Audi and started down the road.

I wasn't Archer. I wasn't going to try and break her door down and I definitely wasn't going to scream at her. I needed her to understand.

This time when I got to the building the inner security door wasn't left conveniently open. My finger hovered over the buzzer with Quinn's name beside it. My heart started racing.

Before I could push on it an older couple walking a small dog left the building. The man opened the door and I took it from him. "Here, let me get that for you," I said.

They thanked me and left, leaving me holding the inner security door open. I went through and soon stood in front of Quinn's door.

I knocked.

The peephole went dark and I knew she was on the other side, looking out at me. She stayed there for a while, probably trying to figure out what to do. I wasn't going to say I knew she was there, I wasn't going to hammer on her door. I gave her time.

The peephole brightened again, signaling that she'd moved away from it. For a few heart-stopping moments I thought that she'd decided to ignore me.

But then the deadbolt shot back with a sharp metal sound and she opened the door a few inches. The chain kept it from going any more. I nodded, accepting that.

"What are you doing here?" she said. "I don't want to see you right now."

I stepped back, not wanting to crowd her. *I am* not *like Archer.*

I nodded to that, too. "I understand. But I know that if I don't see you now, you'll make up your mind for good and decide that you never want to see me again."

She paused, then said, "Who said I haven't already decided on that?"

"Have you?" I asked.

"I'm still standing here talking to you, aren't I?"

"Yes, with the chain still on like you're afraid I'm going to try and batter my way in there."

She looked at the lock and then back to me. I still found her so beautiful, from her eyes and the way her hair fell to her shoulders. It hurt me deep inside to think that there was a very real chance she would tell me to get lost, never to look at her again.

I could see the hurt in her, too. There was some color in her cheeks. Her eyes looked too wet, and strained. I wanted to make it better. I had to make it better.

"I'm not like him, you know," I said. Neither of us needed to say who *him* referred to.

"Maybe you don't threaten to hit me or try and grab me or tell me how worthless I am, but what you said before makes me feel the same way he made me feel."

"You're right. I had no right to do that. We're so good together, Quinn. I know you know that. I think that deserves a second chance. I think *we* deserve a second chance."

She snorted. "I think you mean that you think *you* deserve a second chance."

"Maybe I do. You say I always manage to surprise you. Maybe I'll surprise you again, and show you that I'm a better person than you think I am right now."

"Then do it. Tell me. Right here, right now," she said.

"Tell you what?" I replied, my heart starting to thrum in my chest, it beat so fast and hard.

"Don't play coy with me. If you're serious about all

185

this you'll do it here and now or I'm closing this door in your face and I don't care how long you stand out there waiting for me."

"Quinn... I..." I started. My collar was too tight around my neck. I tugged at it. I glanced up and down the empty hall.

I looked at her. I wanted to get the words out, I really did. But still they refused to come.

"You know what? That does surprise me," she said, "Because I thought you might actually be able to do it. Hey, before you move on to your next girl, will you do the world a favor and come to terms with your feelings so that you stop hurting people?"

She started closing the door, closing me out from her life.

"Hey! That's not fair. Do you think this is easy for me? Do you know how hard it is to stand here and try to overcome all the inertia I've built up over the years?"

She stopped and gave me a hard look. "You walked away just when things were getting good. You didn't even give us a chance."

I wanted to get angry. I wanted to get so angry. "*You're* the one who walked away."

That gave her pause. "Maybe I did. But Vaughn, this isn't good enough. How do I know that you're not just trying to soothe a guilty conscience, that in another week or month or year the exact same thing won't happen again? Can you guarantee that it won't?"

I looked at her, searching her eyes. She meant it. I wanted to blurt out that yes, I could guarantee it. But could I? Could I, really?

Then I heard someone come up beside me.

"Quinn? Is this a bad time?"

I turned and found myself looking at a woman and two young children, a boy and girl. *The ones she babysits*, I realized. I'd never seen them before this, only ever heard about them when Quinn talked about herself. The mother looked tired, older than she was. But she looked down at her kids with real love.

And the keys looked happy to see Quinn. The boy and the girl looked up at me curiously, wondering who I might be.

"No, Mary, it isn't. He was just on his way out," Quinn said.

"Is this your boyfriend, Quinn?" the little girl asked. She was adorable. "He's so handsome!" She looked up at me again and blushed.

The boy looked between Quinn and me with something approaching jealousy in his eyes.

Someone has a crush, I thought. I didn't blame him.

"Charlie!" Mary said, "I'm sorry. Sometimes she just says things."

"That's okay," I replied, smiling my first genuine smile since that fight with Quinn.

The little girl, Charlie, grabbed the bottom of my jacket and gave it a tug. "So, are you Quinn's boyfriend?"

I looked down at her, and then I looked over at Quinn, who'd undone the chain on her door and now stood leaning against the door frame.

"Why don't you kids come on in? I think there's another box of mac & cheese in the pantry I can make for you," Quinn said, stepping aside and waving the kids in. The little boy frowned at me. Charlie kept looking at me over her shoulder until she rounded the corner.

"You never answered her question," I said.

"No, I didn't," she replied, giving me a level look. Then she turned to Mary. "Another shift?"

"I'm sorry, Quinn. It's just been so hectic lately. They keep calling me in and I can't say no with the mortgage payment coming up…" Mary said, trailing off when she looked at me. Her eyes went down and I knew she was embarrassed.

I wanted to tell her not to be, that there was no shame in working hard for your family. But I didn't know how Quinn would take it, so I stayed quiet.

"Really, it's no problem," Quinn said, "Come pick them up whenever you want."

Mary left. I turned back to Quinn, who hadn't shut the door in my face yet.

"What?" Quinn said, crossing her arms, waiting for me to say something. Probably something about how good a person she was for babysitting those kids. Something she might consider sucking up.

"I'm not done with you," I said, trying a smile to see how it went over.

She searched my eyes and for a moment I thought she might relent. "Tonight, you are. Goodnight, Ward."

She closed the door, leaving me alone in the hallway.

Chapter 24

QUINN

I leaned against the door for a while, listening to the kids turn the TV on in the living room. Then I went up on my tiptoes and looked out the peephole again, wondering if Ward might still be out there.

He wasn't. My first reaction was disappointment. I'd come so close to forgiving him there, and when I realized that it had just made me angry all over again and I'd shut him out.

"Is your boyfriend still here, Quinn?" Charlie said, poking her head around the corner and searching the hallway as though Ward might be hiding beneath the little table where I tossed my keys on the way in and out.

"No, he's gone," I said.

"Oh… He seemed nice," she said.

"Yes, he did seem that way, didn't he?" I replied. Part of me just wanted to forget the whole thing so badly, to start again. But the rest of me, that part of me that had gotten me to dump Archer, to go out and apply to places like C&M kept warning me against it.

He'll just hurt you again, that part of me kept saying. So it was better to struggle with it for a little bit now then to make another mistake and get hurt even more down the line.

It was too much to think about at that moment. So I went and grabbed the mac & cheese to make for the kids.

***

Work the next day mostly involved moving all the things from my corner cubicle to my new office on the floor above. It wasn't a corner unit. And it definitely wasn't as large as Ms. Spencer's office, but it was mine.

Every time I came up with an armload of stuff, I kept stopping in front of the door to admire the nameplate on the door.

Quinn Windsor
Junior Partner

I had to keep reminding myself that that really was my name on the plate, that this wasn't a dream.

I thought I'd miss my cubicle, but after my little outburst at Trish people kept glancing at me when they thought I couldn't see. When I went into a room they quieted down, and didn't look me in the eye. *Do they think I'm going to yell at them, too?*

So no, I didn't miss my cubicle.

I hadn't seen Trish at all that day. Some quiet inquiries revealed that she hadn't quit or anything like that. She must have been lying low.

Anne helped me carry the last of the stuff up from my cubicle. She set the box down on my desk. "Wow! This is awesome. I still so happy that you got the promotion!"

"Me too," I said, sinking down into my chair. I put my hands down flat on the desk, enjoying the coolness of the surface against my palms.

I'd told her a lot about what happened between Ward and me. Even the bit about him showing up at my condo. I tried not to think about him, but everything reminded me of him.

Trish reminded me of him because of what he said to her. Anne reminded me of him because of the way she gushed over him. This office and my nameplate reminded me of him because I knew that it was my success with his account that got me into said office.

If he hadn't insisted that I be the one to manage his

account, I don't know how much longer it would have taken me to get to this point.

And thinking of *that* reminded me that I was *still* in charge of his account, technically. Everywhere I turned, there he was.

"So, how are you doing?" Anne asked. She went and grabbed a bottle of water from the mini fridge in the corner. *Oh yeah, I have a mini fridge now.*

"Fine. Lots of work to do, though. Ms. Spencer gave me another account. There's this pharmaceutical company that wants to farm out some of its marketing…"

"Yes, you're truly a 'Mad Woman.' And no, not how work is doing. How are *you* doing?" Anne said. Her hipster glasses gave her eye roll an extra dose of irony.

"You're talking about him?" I said.

"If by him you mean Vaughn Ward, mister number 17 himself, yes."

"Fine. He hasn't bothered me yet today, anyway," I said.

"So you're totally over him, then? Is that what you're saying?"

"Yeah, sure," I replied, no longer meeting her eyes.

"Oh," she said, walking around the perimeter of my office, stopping for a second to scrutinize my degree, which was the first thing I'd hung on the wall, "So I guess if that's the case, you won't really care that apparently he's left Boston and is now in New York?"

My hands curled into fists against the desk. I was glad that Anne didn't face me so that she couldn't see my expression. "Is that so? Good for him." I wondered if I could thank her for helping me move my stuff up and then ask her to go.

"How does that make you feel?" Anne said, this time turning around to put the question to me.

I shrugged, "Is there a certain way it's supposed to make me feel?"

"Upset, maybe?" she shot back.

191

"There's nothing to be upset about. Don't you have some work to do or something?"

This earned me a laugh. "Probably. There usually is. If there's nothing to be upset about, then why are you upset? Might there be some lingering feelings? Some desire to get things back to the way they were?"

"I gave him his chance. I told you that. He didn't take it." I started to get annoyed that she had taken one of my bottles of water without asking.

"You know, some people might say that you set him up to fail there, putting him on the spot like that. Some people might also say that you should try and meet him halfway, see where he's coming from. That sort of thing."

I stood up, meaning to go to the door and open it to let her out. "And some people seem to have far too much interest in my business."

Her smile turned into a grin, "Just trying to look out for you."

"Thanks," I said, my irritation softening. She wasn't trying to tease me. She wanted to help. "And thanks for helping me get all this up here. But you really should get back to work, otherwise I'll have to start abusing my power to keep you from getting canned."

"I knew this friendship would pay off someday!" Anne replied, sticking her tongue out at me. I returned the gesture. She started for the door.

Before she could open it someone knocked on it. "Ooh, I'll get it! Your first caller in your new office!" Anne said. She pulled it open and then she made an "*Eep!*" sound.

I knew what that sound meant. I froze.

"Hi," Ward said.

Anne turned around, her eyes wide and her eyebrows raised.

"Hi," I said. *What is he doing here?* Suddenly I was conscious of what a mess my office was, with all the boxes sitting around in stacks.

"I'll, uh, go back to that… thing I do here. Work, that's it," Anne said. Ward shifted so that she could squeeze by him.

I knew what she was doing, too. Leaving me alone with him. *What a little schemer*, I thought, wishing that I'd asked her to stay. I took a deep breath to steady myself and then sat down.

Be professional, I thought. *I'm just in charge of his account now.*

"It seemed like we'd left some things unsaid back at your condo," Ward said.

"Really? I don't think…" I started, but then I remembered Anne telling me that I'd set him up to fail before. "Maybe. Aren't you supposed to be in New York?"

He looked so handsome still. The way he left the top few buttons on his shirt undone always drove me wild, and I wondered if that was a calculated move on his part.

Again I wanted to just let things happen, to not push him away. But that voice kept speaking, saying things like, *He'll hurt me again. Don't risk it.*

"I'm exactly where I want to be. I wanted you to know that you're the best thing that's happened to me in a long time. I think that you're beautiful and intelligent," he nodded at the name plate on my door, "And successful, and good at what you do."

Don't smile, don't smile, don't smile, I kept thinking. It was difficult. "So tell me something you haven't told me before," I said.

We both knew what I meant.

He ran a hand through his hair and looked around my office. Again I wished he'd come later, after I'd had a chance to make everything look good.

But it was the pause that got to me. The pause, the hesitation that made that protective voice start squawking in my head again.

"I care about you, a lot," he said, not looking at me. "I want you back."

193

I wanted him back, too. I wanted to run into his arms. I wanted him to shut that door and then sweep everything off my desk so that we could give the office a proper christening.

But that pause, I kept thinking. It was a pause that had my protective said telling me, *It's only a matter of time*.

He looked at me. "It's still a *no*, isn't it?"

Be professional.

I gave him a halting nod. Pressure pushed at the back of my eyes. "Please go," I said.

He left. I wondered if it was for good.

***

"I have to *what?*" I said. I couldn't believe it. I had the phone pressed to my ear, spreadsheets displayed on my monitor.

"He insists that you be there. He says that you're in charge of his account, so he wants you there to get a feel for things," Ms. Spencer said.

"Can I let someone else take over?" I asked, my heart sinking.

"Not on notice this short. Don't worry, it will go well," she said.

"Okay. I'll make sure it does," I said. We hung up and I just had to stare blankly at my monitor for a while.

I can't believe he's doing this to me! It had been a week since he'd showed up unannounced at my office. Just enough time for me to start to settle into a new pattern. A work pattern.

And now he'd called some new press conference for a new product. One that he hadn't bothered informing C&M about. That seemed like him, though. He did like a good surprise.

He was hosting it down at a conference room in the Harbor Hotel, too. And that brought to mind one of the things he'd said to me early on. *I always stay at the Harbor when I'm in Boston.*

Of course you do, I thought. And it was in just under an hour. Definitely nowhere near the amount of time needed to prep one of the other partners on his account. *I* had to handle it. I was sure he set it up that way, too.

What's he playing at? Whatever it was, I'd find out soon enough.

I was almost late, too. There was a lot of traffic getting across town. And that left me flustered and irritated and resentful.

The Harbor was a beautiful old hotel right on the water. It had a great view and when I went inside I could see why Ward liked it so much. I spoke with an auditor who directed me to the right conference room. I had to take a set of stairs and turn down the hall a couple times.

I opened the doors. The sound of a hundred different, semi-whispered conversations buffeted me.

Members of the press crowded the room. At the other end there was a stage set up with a microphone stand on it. A few different camera crews jockeyed for the optimal position.

A few people gave me curious looks, noting my lack of a press pass, but otherwise ignored me.

At least I didn't have to wait long. A pretty blonde in a grey skirt stepped up onto the stage and gave the microphone a few taps that got everyone's attention. "Hello. Thank you all for coming on such short notice. I would like to note that there will *not* be a Q&A period following Mr. Ward's announcement. Please keep that in mind. Please take your seats and Mr. Ward will be on shortly."

Another wave of whispered conversation washed over me as we all shuffled for seats. Most of it was about why he wouldn't allow a Q&A, and what he could possibly be announcing.

I sat down and waited.

Ward stepped up onto the stage a minute later.

Cameras flashed. The camera crews adjusted their equipment. People started murmuring and he held up his hands to quiet them.

He looked good, I noted. I tried to ignore that note. I couldn't ignore the way my heart sped up in my chest, or the way of the memory of him coming to my office surfaced in my mind.

"Thank you all for coming. Don't worry, this will be short. Phoenix Software's newest release is still topping the charts, and promising to stay there for many weeks. And I know that the recent marketing push is a big part of that success. The main person responsible for that push, Quinn Windsor, is here with us today. Will you please come up and join me, Quinn?"

I went rigid. *What is he doing? What is this?* Everyone started talking again, craning their necks and turning in their chairs trying to find the person Ward meant.

And I knew that if I wanted to keep my job at C&M I'd have to go along with it. Haltingly, like a robot, I pushed myself up out of my seat. A few confused journalists snapped some pictures of me. Not knowing what else to do, I waved. My heart wanted to explode out of my chest.

"Don't be shy. Come on up," Ward said.

I made my way down to the stage, walking up the steps. "What are you *doing?*" I said from the side of my mouth, trying not to let my smile falter.

The cameras down below us peered at me. Everyone in the room looked at me, it seemed.

"Showing you how serious I am," he replied.

"*Here?*"

But then our private conversation stopped.

"Quinn was instrumental in the success of that release. She became very important to me, too, and for a while now I've been struggling to find a way to express that to her…"

He took a breath and turned to me. I felt rooted to

the spot. He took my hand and set his eyes on mine. "I love you, Quinn. And I'm not afraid to say it. Not even in front of all these people."

The room seemed to shrink, then. All the people disappeared, all the cameras. There was only Vaughn and me. I searched his eyes, looking for any sign of hesitation, any pause, anything held back.

"Please don't tell me I'm too late," he said.

I swallowed. My throat and chest kept getting tighter. *He means it. He really means it.*

"You're not," I said.

Then he kissed me. I missed the touch of his lips so much. His hands clasped at the small of my back and pulled me against him.

That protective voice in the back of my mind had nothing to say, either.

Someone in the crowd whistled. More cameras flashed. I remembered that we weren't alone. We moved apart, my cheeks burning. I wanted to kill him for doing this so publicly and I wanted to kiss him again at the same time.

He always did like to surprise me. And this was nothing if not shocking.

Part of me started wondering what the senior partners at the firm watching this might be thinking. The rest of me didn't care.

"That private island sounds really great about now," I said, low enough so that the microphone didn't pick it up.

"I was hoping you'd say that." Then he did kiss me again.

EPILOGUE

QUINN

Vaughn was waiting for me in his car at the front of my building. He'd insisted that I could buy anything I needed after we left, but I still wanted to pack a few things. Besides, he owned the jet we were going in. It wasn't going to take off without him.

Also, I wanted to let Mary and the kids know I was going away for a while. I knocked on her door.

She answered and there were tears on her cheeks, her eyes red and puffy.

"Mary? What is it? What happened? Are the kids all right?" I said, wondering what could possibly have gone wrong.

She hugged me, her whole body trembling. I hugged her, then forced her away from me so I could look into her face.

"What is it? Please tell me the kids are okay!"

"They're fine, they're just fine," Mary said.

"Then what is it?"

She grabbed my arms. "Quinn, someone from the bank called me this morning."

Every organ in me seemed to sink to the ground. She worked so hard; she didn't deserve to have her home taken from her. "Oh, Mary…" I started. I meant to tell her that she and the kids could stay with me until she found something else.

"Quinn, *someone paid off my mortgage*. All of it. Differential interest and everything. I said there had to be some kind of mistake. You know, like when someone checks their balance and discovers a million dollars they didn't have before? They said there was no mistake. And they wouldn't tell me who paid it or why, only that it was, in fact, paid. Isn't that *amazing*? Who could have done that? And why?"

It was happy crying, I saw then. Joyful tears. Without that massive mortgage payment she could cut back her hours and spend more time with Alex and Charlie.

"I don't know," I said, "But it is so amazing. I am so happy for you." I pulled her into another hug.

I told her that I was going on vacation and that I'd be gone for a while. Alex and Charlie heard us and came to the door, too.

"Are you going with your boyfriend?" Charlie asked.

"Yes, I am," I said, smiling. Then I looked back to Mary. "You're still going to let me babysit for you, right? I insist."

She smiled at me, then wished me a happy vacation.

Vaughn popped the trunk for me when I came down and I loaded my suitcase into it. I got into the passenger seat and we started towards Logan Airport. He reached over and gave my knee a light squeeze.

"Did you pay off Mary's mortgage?" I asked.

He kept his eyes on the road, stopping us at a red light. "She's the one with the two cute kids in your building, isn't she?"

"Yes. Did you?"

The light turned green and we started off again. He shrugged. "I may have looked into her situation."

"You're wonderful," I said.

"No. You are."

***

VAUGHN

The island was beautiful, and being there reminded me of why I'd bought it. Quinn and I stayed in the beach house, spending every morning and evening watching the sun rise and fall.

It was nice and private, which I liked. We could be as loud as we liked. It was so freeing, too. We both felt like new people. I knew I was, and it was because of her.

I had half a mind to ask her if she just wanted to stay here in this tropical paradise with me forever. And I got a giddy feeling in the pit of my stomach when I thought she might say yes.

I had a great bed in that house, too, and we took advantage of it at every opportunity.

I slid my lips down Quinn's throat, leaving a trail of kisses between her heaving breasts. She tasted so good.

Beads of perspiration dotted her lovely body like dew on a leaf in the morning. Just thinking about how I'd made her work up that sweat left me tingling, wishing I could recharge even faster.

She grabbed my face and pulled it back up so we could kiss. When we parted, she looked into my eyes and said, "I love you, Vaughn."

I put my hand on her chest, feeling the heavy beat of her heart. "I love you, too."

THE END

If you enjoyed this book, you might also enjoy

The Pretend Girlfriend

Confident. Brilliant. Rich. Devastatingly handsome. Aiden Manning seemed to have it all. As naive as I was, when he seemed interested in me, I fell head over heels immediately.

But Aiden Manning's life held a dark side, one that he needed to hide at any cost. That's where I would come in. My trusting nature had caused me to owe money to the wrong people, and Aiden was right there and ready to help, if only I'd help him out as well. Just one signature on a piece of paper, and suddenly I was bound to him. The ground rules I had laid out at the beginning quickly melted away, and I found myself being drawn deeper and deeper into Aiden's life.

However, someone couldn't handle that. An even more powerful figure in Aiden's life would stop at nothing to break the two of us apart. It soon became clear that I might have to sacrifice everything I had to keep the two of us together.

The real question was: *How long could I pretend?*

***

"Winning is hardly the term I would choose. More like fought to a draw. Or maybe a fighting retreat... Why won't you go home, Gwen?"

Something hitched in Gwen's throat. She forced herself to breathe, evenly and deeply. "I told you. I wanted to make sure you were all right..." She reached out to touch his shoulder, but Aiden grabbed her wrist. He squeezed, almost to the point of pain, before relaxing his grip.

"That's not why. Don't lie to me," he said. He still hadn't let go of her wrist. She didn't try to pull it free.

"I don't know what you're talking about," she replied.

She gasped as he pulled her hand close to his mouth. His hot breath washed over her fingers. Gooseflesh crawled up and down her body. Her lips parted. Why was his apartment so hot all of a sudden?

"You do know. And I know. Gwen, I've had to try so hard to hold back. You have no idea how hard it's been."

Gwen barely breathed the word, "What?" All she could concentrate on was how close her fingers were to Aiden's lips.

"But I can't do it anymore. I don't have the strength... Why did you have to insist on staying with me tonight?" he said. His thumb started gently massaging the sensitive skin on the bottom of her wrist. Her heart started thumping in her chest.

Am I asleep? Gwen thought. *I must be asleep.*

"Don't have the strength for what?" she asked.

"To keep myself from doing this..."

Aiden kissed the tip of her forefinger. Then the next,

and the next. His lips slid up the back of her hand, leaving a hot trail behind. When he stopped, he placed her hand against his cheek. His stubble tickled at her palm. His eyes seemed to sparkle in the warm lamplight, and his lips glistened invitingly.

She couldn't help leaning in and kissing him. Her whole body committed to the action, and she felt drawn to him. Some part of her wondered if he would break away, as he had so many times before.

But this time he didn't.

No, this time he pulled her up onto his lap, and she straddled him. The temperature in the room, and inside of her, both already at an all-time high, ratcheted up another ten degrees or so.

His lips relished her mouth, then slid down her chin, and from there, her neck. His stubble prickled her smooth skin, adding another element to the sensation.

"You always smell so nice..." Aiden said, "I need to know how you taste..." His fingers pulled the straps of her sundress and bra down, leaving her shoulders bare so that he could kiss those too.

Heat blossomed in Gwen's stomach and moved down. She couldn't get enough of his kisses. While his mouth busied itself exploring her shoulders, his hands dropped down to the small of her back. Even through the thin material of the dress, she could feel the heat from him soaking into her skin.

And then his hands dropped lower, cupping her bottom, squeezing her with need and appreciation.

52795167R00129

Made in the USA
Lexington, KY
11 June 2016